MOX NIX

a tale of
corporate corruption,
chemical toxicity,
and lusts

By Thomas Haag

Holland, Pennsylvania
2006

Dedicated to the late Dr. Conard,
a superb Philadelphia high school English teacher,
who introduced me to the joy and pain of writing.

"All men kill the thing they love...some strangle with the hands of lust, some with the hands of gold: the kindest use a knife, because the dead so soon grows cold...."

—Oscar Wilde

Table of Contents

Acknowledgments

With gratitude to Mary Jane DiPallo, who somehow turned hundreds of pages of poorly-scripted cursive writing into a legible, if unreadable, manuscript; Justin Bowers, a wunderkind editor; Foster Winans, the gentlemanly founder of the Writers Room of Bucks County, who took me by the hand when I was lost; my wife and daughters, who prodded me to finish the task while providing accurate criticism I found highly irritating; and my parents, who taught me that you can go anywhere, if you just keep putting one foot in front of the other.

The list of human lusts is endless: we lust for life and call it survival instinct; lust for parental approval and call it sibling rivalry; lust for power and call it leadership; lust for status and wealth and call it ambition; lust for carnal pleasure and call it love; lust for immortality and call it faith.

MOX NIX

Prologue

T he Delaware Valley and the city of Philadelphia were the cradle of both the political independence of the United States, and its commercial dependence on the chemical industry. The broad expanse of the Delaware River made the city the largest freshwater port in the Western Hemisphere. Here, in this fertile seventeenth-century marketplace, the raw materials and political ideals of freedom of the New World were exchanged for the manufactured goods and intellectual ideas of the Old World. Unlike other colonies, religious and personal freedoms flourished under the wise governance of William Penn, long before they were drafted in the eighteenth century into the Declaration of Independence and the Constitution.

The desire to add value to the New World's abundant raw materials gave birth to the chemical industry. The woods teemed with wildlife, so shipyards and tanneries sprung up along the banks and tributaries of the river. Downstream, on the Brandywine Creek, a man named DuPont started a gunpowder mill.

Natural but odiferous chemicals employed in the tanning process, such as fermented dog feces, soon exiled the leather factories from the city to places such as Bridesburg to the north, where the Frankford Creek merged with the Delaware.

By 1882 there were thirty-eight chemical plants in the city of Philadelphia, and many more arrayed north and south along the river banks.

In the nineteenth century, Otto Von Bismark created his "Ein Deutschland" from a hodge-podge of small, weak duchies and principalities. He used three tools: war, peace, and education. Once he had consolidated his territorial claims for the new Germany, the "Iron Chancellor of War" sought to ensure European peace while building Germany into a unified, socially progressive, industrialized nation, laced with roads, canals, railroads, and technically-advanced factories.

He emphasized superior education and academic excellence, encouraging German workers to advance their skills through a formal apprentice, journeyman, and meister training process. One of the fields in which Germany leapt ahead was chemistry, establishing a lead so great that other nations, including the U.S., required proficiency in German to qualify for a degree.

Early in the twentieth century, the robust American leather industry merged with German chemical excellence when a shrewd German entrepreneur, Hans Schopfer, met a brilliant research chemist, Doktor Friedrich Reiner. The latter had invented synthetic chemical compounds to improve the tanning process, and Hans was just the man to manufacture and market them. Recruiting a highly-trained, technical sales force, Hans's field representatives could go into tanneries and demonstrate the usefulness and value of the technology, securing the high prices and profits required to support more research by Doktor Reiner. Out of this dynamic partnership a major twentieth century chemical company was born—Schopfer Chemical—requiring Hans to emigrate from Germany to Bridesburg to establish the American Division.

By the 1960s, the Schopfer Chemical Building stood at the corner of what would later become Philadelphia's Independence Mall. Schopfer then made a major commitment to the redevelopment of the area, which had decayed after World War II into a jumble of dilapidated buildings, small businesses, bus depots, and flop houses. It was later joined by the Federal Mint, IRS, court house complex, refurbished office buildings, a TV studio, and tourist facilities for visitors to the Liberty Bell and the old Pennsylvania State House, where the Declaration of Independence and the Constitution were drafted.

The Schopfer building represented an act of faith and commitment by Hans Schopfer to his adopted city; a monument to the Horatio Alger ideal of great success stemming from great labors, foresight, and daring; a monument to progress based on science in general, and more specifically, chemistry; and a triumph of the system of capitalism and free enterprise which Hans had eagerly embraced.

In just fifty years, he had parlayed a single product, an idea, and twenty-five thousand dollars into an industrial giant employing thousands in high-paying jobs. Schopfer was in one of the few industries with a surplus in international balance of payments. It had played a key role in helping win World War II, made products which eased and enriched the lives of millions, and quietly funded large charitable foundations. But to its critics in the age of environmentalism, it was a rapacious corporation exploiting the public while poisoning the land, water, and air.

When Hans died in 1962, his two sons, Ernst and Robert, inherited control of Schopfer, ranked in the middle of the Fortune 500. Ernst immediately set about putting his personal stamp on the business, abandoning the fiscal conservatism of his Old World father. Ernst was under pressure, in the atmosphere of the go-go years, to stimulate rapid growth by investing in diverse industries and new, high-risk technologies. His brother, Robert, assumed a largely ceremonial role, serving as head of administration, personnel, and advertising, while indulging his passion for good social works and his role as patron of the arts.

They both enjoyed plush offices with sweeping views of Independence Mall and the vast waterfront stretching to the Atlantic Ocean and the world beyond. To the north they could see plumes of smoke pouring from steel mills, power plants, factories, and chemical plants. The belching stacks dwarfed the surrounding church spires, spewing clouds of prosperity that obscured trouble brewing just beneath the surface.

Chapter One

Two Roads To Travel

Harry Schoen checked his wristwatch to make sure he'd left enough time to get to his meeting with the workers' council. He locked his desk and then emptied all of the Schopfer Chemical Company work papers from his attaché case. He placed them in a large envelope along with his desk key, sealed it, put a strip of scotch tape over the sealed edge, printed "Company Confidential" on the face and back, and wrote his secretary's name on the front. He penned a brief note to his secretary and placed it in a business envelope marked "Personal."

He placed a few photographs and trinkets from his desk drawers in the empty attaché and pushed the locking latches. He stood and walked to the windows of his expansive corner office on the next-to-top floor of the Schopfer Chemical Building, facing the Independence Hall Mall. As they had been for months, Vietnam War protestors could be seen swarming far below like ants. To Harry they were just the latest in a long string of protest groups that had become part of the urban scene. They had lost even their curiosity value. He had other things on his mind. He gazed northward toward the Bridesburg section of the city, where his evening's mission would end.

It had been a tumultuous year. It reminded him of the intensity of his experiences in Korea, except that in combat you could tell by the uniforms who was friend and who was foe, and the objective was clear: kill or be killed. Like Tom Rath, the unhappy 1950s corporate executive played by Gregory Peck in "The Man in the Gray Flannel Suit," Harry had returned from his battlefield experiences eager to trade his khakis in for the uniform of business—blue pinstripes, wing-tipped shoes, and university-striped ties. Like Rath, he had discovered that corporate warfare, in which all combatants look the same, was a treacherous endeavor where your opposition was in front of you, and your enemies behind your back.

He had been a rising star at Schopfer—Harry "the pretty," as anyone who understood the English translation of his German surname might have called him. He was guided in his career by the codes of his parents. His father's message: "The coward dies a thousand deaths, the brave man but one." From his Irish mother, it was that no one makes you a victim without your consent. Together they imbued him with liberal ideas—to inflict pain without purpose is immoral, and to be true to himself—and encouraged him to be considerate with people.

He'd been raised with no more powerful moral compass than that. He was at best a "sprinkle" Christian: sprinkled with water when christened, with rice when married, and expected to be sprinkled with dirt when dead. Between the water and the dirt, he had encountered plenty of mud, but the rice had not flourished.

Now Harry paused at the office door to set his face for his final departure from the building. It had been ten months since he'd stood on the front steps of the Schopfer building on his way to meet Marie. It seemed like a lifetime ago.

———•••••———

Harry had hesitated that previous June afternoon at the top of the steps to let his eyes adjust to the glare. His tailored gabardine suit was no match for the oppressive heat and humidity. He pulled his handkerchief from its perch in his breast pocket and mopped the beads of sweat that were forming on his upper lip. At Independence Hall, across busy Sixth Street, work crews were putting the finishing touches on the promenades and greenery of the new mall. He allowed himself a moment of self-satisfaction. Schopfer had played an important role in lobbying for redevelopment of the area. It had come a long way from the shabby buildings and Franklin Square derelicts he'd mingled with in his teen years working as a teamster loading trucks at the old Whitman Chocolate Factory on Race Street.

The decrepit buildings had been razed and the vagrants herded north and west, compressed into the tenderloin of Vine Street on the edge of Chinatown, where modern-day religious missionaries made the drunks and the derelicts sing hymns for their suppers. Now the industrious Chinese immigrants, already besieged by highway projects and wholesale urban renewal projects on the one side, were hemmed in on the other by the human debris that had been flushed uptown and onto their doorsteps.

This day Harry did not, as was his habit, join the flow of commuters turning west on Market Street toward the railroad terminals. Instead, he became part of the small eddy drifting eastward toward the stinking Delaware River.

High above the city, in his office in the Schopfer Building, Robert Schopfer gazed down on the shimmering cityscape and spotted Harry, noting his departure with passing curiosity. Robert, as usual, had run out of things to do by the end of his "work" day and had given his papers a final, bored reshuffling. He knew Harry was hosting an engagement party for his daughter, Babs, that evening. But Harry was leaving work headed in the wrong direction. He shrugged off the thought, and then remembered to write a note for his secretary to make sure the travel agent had booked tickets for his family's summer vacation in Scotland.

Harry passed the old Christ Church burial ground, glancing at Ben Franklin's grave through the iron grating, walked down a narrow colonial alley and slipped into a small bar. He paused to let his eyes adjust to the dimness, drinking in the pleasant, manly atmosphere of stale beer, tobacco smoke, and olives—a refreshing change from the sterile workplace. He made a furtive survey of the bar's few occupants, reassuring himself that this would be a quiet, unobtrusive spot where a discreet conversation would go unnoticed.

Harry exchanged nods with the bartender, who

was already pouring the scotch for his usual dry Rob Roy. He waited at the rail while the bartender expertly filled the glass to the rim, and set it on the bar without spilling a drop.

Marie watched Harry from her banquette seat, stirring her drink with one hand and touching her gray-splashed hair with the other. She felt a tingle of excitement as she watched him wend his way toward her between the tables, like a cat disdainfully avoiding puddles. She loved tall men, and she liked the way his crisp English-style suit defined his slim physique.

She liked just about everything about Harry—the dash of salt at the temples of his dark hair, his dark eyes, straight nose, and ruddy skin—very Arabesque. It was a shame, she sometimes thought, that when his hair was tousled, his suit removed, and his incipient middle-age paunch revealed, his spirit seemed weary and he wasn't all that handsome. She assumed he thought the same of her. They had that, and much more, in common.

Marie was drawn toward successful men, or at least toward the success of men. It was more than the smell of money. Accomplishment attracted her. Maybe it was the same emotion at work when cavemen used to impress their mates by clubbing prey and presenting the pelts to win sexual favors. Marie could appreciate the animal attraction of a gorgeous janitor or repairman, but she saved her true passion for a newly-appointed, fast-rising divisional sales manager like Harry had been when they'd first met in her boss's office three years earlier.

Her interest was not instant. In fact, her first reaction was antagonistic. She was a Girl Friday, loyal as a German Shepherd to her charismatic boss, Charley Winston, and had sensed the competitive danger Harry posed to the senior man. But Harry had that certain something she found hard to resist, the pheromone of ambition perhaps, and later was annoyed with herself at the power of her attraction and—after a long period of nearly perfect celibacy, both preceding and following her husband's death—the speed of her surrender. In fact, she surprised herself by making the first subtle moves to initiate the affair.

Harry slid into the booth with a soft, "Hi." They smiled simultaneously, lifted by each other's presence, especially at the end of a used-up Friday afternoon. Harry placed his hand lightly over hers. They sipped and chatted, more absorbed in each other than in gossip and banality.

Marie sighed lightly and looked at him with a raised eyebrow. "Sure you can't stay in town for a few hours?"

He squeezed her hand and shrugged. "Nancy's putting on a barbecue and splash bash for the neighbors, and now that Babs suddenly decided to announce her engagement, the number of guests blew up. Even Robert and Zelda Schopfer are attending. Things are bad enough between Nancy and me. If I arrive late..."

Marie stared into her drink, swirling the ice. "It wasn't fair to ask, but it's been a little while. I miss you."

"Hey, I miss you too." He patted her hand. "But you know how swamped we've been at the office with this damn reorganization and all the personnel evaluations that have to be updated, God only knows why. But let's settle on something for next Thursday. In fact, we'll make it elegant—dinner at the Emperor, cocktails, wine, and a two-million calorie dessert. Afterwards, if you play your cards right, you might be able to seduce me—several times."

She brightened. "In that case, you better get some rest before Thursday." Harry chortled, his teeth brilliantly white against his summer tan. He gave her a light kiss on the cheek and stood to go. "Oh," she remembered, "any word on Charley's promotion?"

"No, but I have a meeting on Monday and I'll probe it a little. Maybe I'll have more news for you Thursday."

———•◦•———

Harry rode the train home to Bucks County enjoying the glow he always got from Marie's strong response to him. He found her incredibly stimulating, especially in contrast to the cool remoteness of his wife, Nancy. Marie was seven years older than he, which seemed to bother her considerably. She dieted and exercised faithfully, and her clothes and hair styles were up to date with the latest fashion. She had been widowed with little money, but had set her course, graduating from a good business school, eventually going back to work. She worked her way up to executive secretary while learning to manage her own household affairs and raising her only child, Donald, now stationed in Japan as a career Air Force officer. Harry was only thirteen years Donald's senior. When Harry had commented that Donald's photograph bore a striking resemblance to himself, Marie quickly disagreed.

By the time he drove up to the house, the warmth of Marie's attention had dissipated and been replaced with the customary dread he felt about the evening ritual. How eagerly he had looked forward to arriving at their first cramped apartment, with a smiling Nancy to greet him. By the time they bought their first suburban rancher, they had fallen into the gray-flannel pattern of men like himself, bringing home a litany of work frustrations that competed over cocktails and dinner with the litany of domestic problems delivered by his frowning wife. Now, when he arrived at their spacious colonial on five lush acres, he hoped she might be out on an errand so he could mix himself a highball and enjoy a quiet stroll around the grounds.

———◦•◦•◦———

At the moment Harry motored into his driveway, Lorraine Zdanowski stepped out the door of her cramped rowhouse in the Bridesburg section of Philadelphia. She and her neighbors lived in the shadow of Schopfer Chemical's main plant, just beyond the gate at the end of the block where several towering smoke stacks belched the by-product of prosperity. Just beyond, she could see the upper half of an ore ship gliding majestically up the channel in the broad Delaware River on its way to dock and unload at the sprawling U.S. Steel plant a few miles north. No matter how many times she saw it, Lorraine enjoyed the bizarre illusion of an ocean-going ship traveling along a city street.

Lorraine's father had worked at the Bridesburg plant all his life, before his cancer-corroded lungs finally gave out. He had been widowed when Lorraine was twelve, and she had been thrown into the roles of homemaker and of mother to Stosh, her younger brother. Her father's death had eclipsed her hopes for college, and dreams of teaching elementary school. Like many of her neighbors, her first stop had been at the Schopfer personnel office where she was hired into the typing pool. Bright and agreeable, she had rapidly advanced to become secretary to the plant manager.

To the majority of the residents of Bridesburg, Schopfer was a good neighbor offering generations of their families secure, benevolent employment. Company loyalty was so high that union organizers had failed in their repeated attempts to fully organize the plant workers for whom the benevolence of old Hans during the Depression, when he refused to lay off a single employee, was legendary.

With unusual purpose, Lorraine made her way to the bus which would carry her to the Frankford El—the elevated rail line. She disembarked in the tunnel complex under City Hall and changed to the Broad Street subway to travel a few blocks north where she had an appointment in the tall white building that was her destination, the home of the *Philadelphia Times*, one of the city's daily newspapers. She checked her appearance in the lobby mirror before presenting herself to the receptionist, who directed her to the correct floor for columnist Willis Brophy.

———◆•••◆———

Harry Schoen's wife, Nancy, bustled about the kitchen in a prickly mood. Marcy, the part-time maid from Alabama, was languidly washing and chopping salad ingredients and placing them in a huge wooden bowl.

"Marcy, please hurry with that salad. We still have the hors d'oeuvres to prepare." Without looking up, Marcy muttered softly, "Yes, ma'am."

Through the kitchen window, Nancy could see her youngest daughter Babs, short for Barbara, stringing Japanese lanterns between the trees in front of the swimming pool. Nancy loved the romantic soft light they cast, enough for dining and just the right mood for dancing into the evening. She felt a familiar stab of pain cross her brow, as she often did when stressed. What had started out as an informal splash party and barbecue for a few neighbors and friends had escalated into a major social event when Babs made a last-minute decision to use it as a forum to announce her engagement.

Nancy had no choice but to add relatives and old friends to the guest list, as well as some of Babs's friends and their partners. The count had expanded from eight to twenty-four. On top of that, Harry had casually mentioned the affair to Robert Schopfer, expecting a polite decline. But Robert promptly accepted. Nancy had been to a Christmas party and several other social occasions at Robert and Zelda's Main Line mansion. She was a perfectionist and it was important to her feeling of self-worth and acceptance to make a strong statement. She felt she had suddenly found herself under the gun. A relaxing evening with a few close friends had become a major performance that would be judged.

Nancy was grateful that Marcy was available to work, and that Nancy's married daughter, Ellen, had been able to pitch in, although she had insisted, out of her concern for her daughter's third month of pregnancy, that Ellen rest periodically.

Nancy rubbed the spot on her forehead that now throbbed.

"Damn, I wish Harry would get home," she grumbled. "He's got to pick up more liquor and the shrimp and clams at the shopping center."

Marcy nodded and tried to be reassuring. "Now don't you worry. Mistah Schoen, he'll get home in time and he'll barbecue those beef roasts just right, and mix-up those great cocktails of his." Marcy smiled to herself. She admired "Mistah Schoen" so, and loved his sense of humor. He always joked that he was her boyfriend, and always went through an elaborate ritual of having her act as official taste consultant for his cocktails. He often surreptitiously slipped her a few extra drinks in a milk bottle secreted in a paper bag, and on days when Nancy had been especially difficult to deal with, tucked a ten-dollar bill in the bag.

Nancy glanced at Marcy's back as the maid stood at the sink, hitching up her drooping panties over her ample hips. Nancy groused to herself, "Yes, damn it—good old Harry, he can do anything. I slave all day and he'll splash some wine sauce on the beef while it's barbecuing, throw together some drinks and everyone will think he's great." She used to enjoy basking in the light Harry seemed to generate, but that was a long time ago. Over the years, their relationship had degenerated into an elaborate charade for the children, relatives, neighbors, and business associates. But she was addicted to the perquisites of his success, flashing her diamonds and cuddling her furs as she motored to social meetings in her new Cadillac coupe.

She was proud of having ascended to vice-chair of the Ladies Club of Yardley and belonging to the country club. And she felt secure in her position now that it looked like Harry was ascending another notch on the corporate ladder, to where stock options began and he could expect an increase in salary plus a large bonus.

But she saw herself as an intelligent, independent person and yearned to be viewed as more than a help-mate. Nancy had always felt insecure even as she pushed herself into her community activities, while Harry had become more confident and self-reliant—to the point that she had grown resentful of his smug assurance. Whatever the problem, he could handle it. The demands of his job had increased yearly, and the extensive travel thrust much of the day-to-day responsibilities of home life on her. She was the good trooper at first, bravely smiling good-byes and hellos to help him further his career, but then self-pity crept in. She increasingly took to harping to Harry about the problems she had to solve each day.

She often claimed to be too tired to welcome him sexually. Harry had struggled to warm her up with thoughtful acts and gifts. He craved sex as a release for the emotions he had to hold under rigid control in his business life. But he realized that she was exercising her ability to punish him for his career absorption. Their couplings became less and less frequent and more and more the result of animal urges and accidental contact during sleep. Nancy and Harry no longer made love. They had occasional sex.

By treating him coldly, Nancy amplified her problem by driving Harry away when she actually wanted his warmth. She failed to see that by becoming an immovable object she was deflecting his irresistible force in another direction. Harry, in turn, invested that much more into the emotional strait-jacket of his career. It left him vulnerable to Marie when she offered the open ear, the inviting smile, and the warm bed where he could achieve the escape he craved from his emotional cage.

Under the cover of convenience, Harry had moved three weeks ago into Ellen's old bedroom where his early morning starts and frequent late arrivals wouldn't disturb Nancy. In explaining it to Babs, he'd said, "After all, why should your mother have to be awakened at five o'clock when she doesn't have to catch the 6:02, and I don't even bother much with breakfast anymore. She's gotten up enough mornings and lost enough sleep at night when you and your sister were children. She works hard to run this house, and she needs her rest." Babs had accepted her father's rationale with a broadly mugged leer, a wink, and an elbow to her father's ribs. "I guess I'll hear a lot of pitter-patter up and down the old hallway at nights!"

When Harry announced the move, Nancy feigned indifference, but inside she felt chilled. He had presented it as a fait accompli, not a suggestion. It might mean the extinction of the remaining flicker of passion between them. Harry was still a virile, if less urgent, male. She didn't want to end up as several of her friends recently had: divorced and bored, with reduced finances and social standing. Even though she received the news coolly, Nancy realized that she required a good screw on a regular basis, and she hadn't had one since Harry switched bedrooms.

As she prepared to dress for the party, she pulled on her robe and then threw it open again as she posed left and right before the full-length wall mirror. "Not too bad old gal, not bad at all," she mused aloud. True, her pubic hair did not match the shade on her head. True, the middle was a little too thick—but only about four or five pounds, she observed expertly. Nothing that couldn't be starved off before the full bathing suit and tennis season. Her breasts were a little low, but she noted with satisfaction that they were still full and well-rounded. There was a slight dimpling of the skin on the upper legs and a few small spider veins, but overall she rated herself as a well-shaped and conditioned forty-two-year-old. She cupped a breast to rate its firmness and withdrew her hand suddenly upon feeling the rapid hardening of the nipple. She hastily tied the robe closed.

Chapter Two

Home Sweet Home

Harry tiptoed into the kitchen, startling Marcy by grabbing her ample waist. Marcy jumped and then giggled as she recognized her assailant. "Lord sakes, Mistah Schoen!"

Harry laughed and winked conspiratorially. "Come on, Marcy, you know you're hot for my body."

"Oh, Mistah Schoen," she protested, shaking her head reprovingly.

Harry leaned out the kitchen door and called to Babs, "Hey princess, come on in and have a cocktail with your broken-down old dad."

Babs waved and bounded toward the door, planting a peck on her father's cheek. "Oh, Daddy! Those whiskers of yours hurt!"

He turned and loudly addressed Marcy, who was surreptitiously enjoying the scene, "When she was a little girl, she used to say that she wanted to feel my 'wires.' Now they hurt. But I'll bet Robbie's whiskers don't bother her!"

His daughter Ellen entered and crossed the room to give him a kiss and hug, deliberately rubbing her cheek against his. Harry exaggeratedly pushed his fanny out and said in mock seriousness, "Ellen doesn't stand as close as she used to."

Ellen beamed and blushed. "I haven't even begun to show."

He patted her on the fanny. "You just take good care of that grandchild of mine." He placed his arms about his daughters' waists. "Come on ladies, let me escort you to the bar for something tall and cool." They were marching off toward the recreation room bar when Nancy appeared in her robe.

"Harry," she spoke rapidly, "it's good you're here. I have a list for you to do. Ellen, you lie down again. Babs, please finish the lanterns and put the towels in the cabana." Marcy returned to her salad.

"Okay, girls. We'll have our drink later, when we're ready for the party."

Nancy found Harry's good humor exasperating and proceeded to engage him in brittle conversation. "Harry, you've got to hurry over to the liquor store for more vermouth. And don't forget the grenadine. Stop at the market for the shrimp and clams. Mix the manhattans, martinis, and a small container of pink ladies." For Zelda, Robert Schopfer's wife—Nancy was an excellent hostess who remembered such details.

"Drive Marcy home, and please wear your new burgundy slacks and white blazer. I laid them out for you."

"Yes sir!" He nodded and gave a crisp military salute while clicking his heels.

Dusk began to gather as Harry entered the screened patio, his errands complete and his chef's duties in progress. The beef roasts, which had been turning on the barbecue for some time, were beginning to give off a rich aroma. Harry was satisfied that all appeared attractive and serene—belying the frantic preparations. The lanterns at poolside glowed softly, as did the candles on the patio. The strains of Frank Sinatra's "My Way" echoed throughout the house, while three of the four women in his life sat on the glider, dressed in the highly-designed "casual" clothes that had cost him a fortune. Harry was about to join them when he heard the first car crunching up the driveway. He cupped his hands and called, "Battle Stations."

In under an hour the party was in full swing. Most of the appetizers had disappeared and a steady flow of alcohol had lubricated the guests. The usual suburban conversations were in progress: "Damn taxes! Has the school board gone crazy, putting in an Olympic pool?" "Now George, it really isn't an Olympic pool, and besides..." "Do you know that the planning commission is actually considering allowing low-cost housing in the county?" "And the identical dress was on sale in town for twenty dollars less!"

Harry artfully basted the roasts with his signature wine sauce and drifted into his alone-in-the-crowd melancholia. It usually began when he had some alcohol in him, but not enough to really permit his spirit to be freed of inhibitions. In such a state, Harry tended to become a too-keen observer of others, rather than a participant. He realized that he did not have one true friend in the crowd. This was partly his own fault. His standards for friendship were lofty and he held himself aloof and reserved with most people, until he knew them well.

Nancy played a role as well, discouraging Harry from staying in touch with most of his pre-marital friends. She couldn't help feeling jealous of his past good times and it was her way of exercising control. Harry was now encircled by Nancy's selection of friends, many of whom Harry regarded as pretentious strivers. He spotted Charley Winston, his benevolent boss and mentor, and smiled at Charley's alcohol-fueled antics and gestures.

Babs's friends began dancing poolside. Nancy danced with John Warden, their neighbor and family lawyer. She glowed with beauty and her bright smile caused Harry a pang of sorrow over their chilly relationship. Nancy seemed taken with John and Anne Warden, probably because of their wealth and social connections. Babs danced dreamily with her fiancé, Robbie, with her head on his shoulder and eyes nearly closed. Could have done a lot worse, Harry mused. He has a good future as an insurance salesman in his father's agency, even though he dropped out of college in his junior year. He looks decent and seems to be a sensible kid.

"What's the problem, Harry? I thought I was going to be the only pensive person tonight." He turned to face Bobby Schopfer. "Perhaps the father is realizing that his little girl isn't a little girl anymore."

"You may be right, Robert, but I'm sure I'll recover."

"I've gone through that experience twice myself, you know." Bobby grinned crookedly, awkwardly patting Harry on the shoulder. It was a feeble but valiant attempt at a human gesture, the best he could manage with a male other than his brother Ernst.

Harry was embarrassed to see Bobby's eyes glistening slightly. Then he mumbled a comment about the smoke and moved away toward his wife, Zelda, who was sitting with Anne Warden, the wife of Nancy's dance partner, John. Anne had been born into great wealth and high social standing. She was also born with a natural empathy for others, and often spent her time at parties like this one seeing that no one felt lonely or unimportant.

Bobby paused and glanced back at Harry before continuing toward Zelda. "Yes Harry, this will be a major occasion for you, perhaps in several ways." He grinned his crooked grin again and walked away.

Harry returned to his basting but his mind was racing, trying to connect dots—raised eyebrows, word inflections, inappropriate pauses in conversations when Harry arrived to join in. The management committee was to meet on Tuesday. There had been a number of closed-door meetings among senior executives. Personnel files were being updated. The VP of marketing would be retiring soon.

Suddenly the math seemed to add up: Charley Winston will become the assistant VP for Marketing! Ben Jensen will retire and Jack Boswelth, the present assistant VP, would move up. One of the divisional sales managers would take Charley's place as General Manager—it would be Harry.

He immediately discounted the idea, but then it crept back into his thoughts. When his brain performed its mysterious machinations, it was frequently correct.

His spontaneous analyses had gained accolades from his colleagues: "penetrating insights, original thinker, clever fellow, creative." He operated on intuition, rather than as a constructor of syllogisms, deductive and inductive processes.

His brow furrowed at a second thought: How much influence had his relationship with Robert had on his promotion, if it were to be made? He had been a reverse snob on this point, making it a hard rule not to play office politics by socializing with and kissing up to the people for whom he worked.

Harry's relationship with Bobby was sympathetic. He felt sorry for the shy, gentle, misfit executive in the jungle of a highly-competitive industry. He harbored a protective affection for Bobby, much as he would have toward a reticent but honest child. Bobby, meanwhile, had become infected by Harry's enthusiasm, one of Harry's innate characteristics—he was the complete salesman, selling himself on projects, and then projecting his excitement to others. For Bobby, any emotion gave him a rush, a welcome contrast to the reserved, cool style that prevailed among the staff in the office.

There was a bit of a hero worship in Bobby's admiration for Harry, a well-decorated combat veteran of Korea, particularly in contrast with his own privileged background. Bobby seemed to enjoy basking in Harry's light and made sure to invite the Schoens to the elegant charity events they frequented, and Harry and Nancy dutifully reciprocated, although in more modest fashion, such as a quiet evening of Bridge.

In the work environment, the two men met occasionally for lunches where they chewed over minor business topics.

Harry welcomed but did not court Bobby's tentative advances, anxious to avoid appearing to use their acquaintance for personal gain. For his part, Bobby—like a plain-looking heiress—had developed an instinct for detecting attempts to exploit him, and appreciated Harry's sense of decorum and distance. Harry had a knack for giving Bobby the feeling that he was being accepted for himself, not for what he could provide.

Harry's belief system, honed during his years in the Army, was based on performance—if you got the job done, your reward would follow. It was not lost on him that less able men received promotions faster than he. But over time he saw most of them stumble or fail when their lack of skills or tools were exposed by poor performance.

Harry's officer-and-gentleman code of conduct had served him well among the troops in the lower and middle management ranks. But there were other rules at work in the upper levels. When he realized what was required, he had joined the country club, and sharpened his bridge, tennis, and golf games. He allowed himself limited forays into the social swirl of the executive class.

He'd felt clumsy and uneasy, since he'd had to make a wholesale change in lifestyle—bigger house and all of that—and in his social life. He had allowed his ties to old friends and neighbors, whom he genuinely liked, to wither. He'd had to hold his nose in order to violate his belief in political and social meritocracy.

Harry's ascent had put an even greater strain on Nancy, forcing her to adapt to an alien social environment for which she was ill-equipped. After just one year of college, she'd forfeited the rest of her education to wed Harry. Instead she went to work while he pursued his MBA. Forsaking their old friends and neighbors when they moved into a more affluent area bothered both Nancy and Harry.

Harry and Nancy's pool party was aging nicely. The food had been consumed, the candles burned lower, and most of the guests were now dancing or had formed small, quiet conversational clutches. A few of Babs's friends had changed into suits and gone for a swim. The Schoens, the Schopfers, and the Hawthornes, Babs's future in-laws, had gathered into one group. Zelda Schopfer was gushing about her latest charitable activity—a largely black boys club in north Philly's ghetto. Babs and Robbie strolled up. Babs smiled and placed a hand on Harry's shoulder. "Excuse me, please, but could you make the announcement now before your friends go to sleep, or my friends disappear into the bushes?"

Harry marveled at the way she radiated happiness. He smiled at Robbie. "Not before I perform one last duty," he began, in a mockingly serious tone. "Robbie, are you really sure you know what you're doing?" Robbie nodded and grinned broadly, looking at Babs for confirmation.

"Okay, you've named your poison." Harry stood up and, in a resonant voice that had once commanded soldiers in combat, called for quiet. When the scattered chattering had died away, he began, "Friends, neighbors, family, lend me your ears. As most of you know from experience, marriage is the worst form of coexistence between male and female—save for any other. However, my daughter Babs and Robbie Hawthorne have decided to become engaged and begin the arduous preparations for a marriage in September. I sincerely welcome the addition of the Hawthornes to our family circle, as Nancy and I find them to be most agreeable people."

The obligatory round of applause, hugs, kisses, back slaps and laughter followed. Harry and Nancy stood in a loose embrace, for the moment the happy, united parents. Harry allowed himself to wallow in a bit of nostalgia to go along with his melancholia. This rare bit of public intimacy with Nancy put a warm smile on his face, and a warm glow in his heavy heart.

"Could I have your attention please!" Bobby Schopfer's shrill voice cut through the babble. In a festive mood now, it took a little longer to get the assemblage to quiet down.

Bobby had a smile on his face and a gleam in his eye that Harry didn't recognize. He felt a trickle of adrenaline course through his veins.

"I think it's appropriate to make a two-part toast at this time, one to Babs' and Mr. Hawthorne's future happiness, and the second to Mr. Harry Schoen for his promotion to Assistant VP for Marketing of Schopfer Chemical!"

Harry felt a jolt of electricity that made his eyes blink so hard he couldn't see for a moment. Then Bobby stepped forward through the crowd and shook his hand, his eyes wide with pleasure, a manic grin on his face. Nancy squeezed Harry around the waist and kissed him gently on the cheek. Softly she breathed, "Congratulations, darling."

A blur of applause, hoots, and vigorous hand-shaking followed. Harry was, for one of the few times in his life, nearly stumped, and began to stammer a thank-you. He'd been caught completely by surprise.

"Imagine that! A tongue-tied sales executive," quipped a voice from the rear. Out of the blur of flushed, happy faces, Harry caught a still-life image of Charley Winston and his wife Agnes, wearing frosty smiles. Harry had been leap-frogged right over Charley. Harry's code of conduct demanded that he rush to console them, but he was held captive by the mob of well-wishers.

The headlights of the last departing car swept the patio and were gone. The soft music, which had disappeared into the background for most of the revelry, now provided a mellow coda, accompanied by the crickets, as a Jackie Gleason arrangement, featuring the full trumpet of Billy Butterfield, floated like a mist across the garden. Nancy moved with heavy footsteps around the tables, gathering glasses and napkins on a tray.

"Let it go," Harry insisted. "I asked Marcy to come in the morning and handle all this, and I'll put the grounds back in order tomorrow after breakfast."

"Thanks. That was thoughtful. I'm beat."

He stubbed his cigarette out in an ashtray, stood

and stretched. "That makes two of us. I'm going to turn in. You were a splendid hostess. You looked very attractive. That new outfit is very smart."

Nancy smiled and curtsied, "Thank you, kind assistant VP and future VP and member of the board. Seriously, I'm very happy for you."

"Thanks. Rest well. I'll see you in the morning."

"Harry?" He paused. "Remember how we used to celebrate your promotions?" He rubbed the side of his nose, an unconscious tic from childhood. Nancy's previous rejections had done their cumulative damage and aroused a narrow streak of Teutonic cruelty. He was at heart loyal and moral and had suffered when he had first begun to be unfaithful. By twisted logic, he now felt respectable again by being faithful to Marie. He considered Nancy's clumsy attempt at seduction to have been triggered by her looming loss of Babs, and the aphrodisiac effect of his new promotion, which would elevate her social status. It seemed like an empty gesture.

"That was a long time ago," he said softly as he turned and walked into the house.

Nancy looked away as tears began to well. He had never rejected her before. The hot flush of humiliation quickly transformed itself into anger. "Bastard!" she hissed. "You rotten bastard." She shakily poured herself a heavy dose of whiskey and sucked down a hefty draft. The alcohol couldn't keep the shaking from radiating through the rest of her body.

Was this a sign post along the route to divorce? Harry had been a virile lover, more highly sexed than she. How could he deny his passion? Was he denying it? She polished off the rest of her drink in one long, thirsty gulp.

Chapter Three

Two Views From The Top

Robert Schopfer stood at the window of his office staring out over the city and noticed his reflection in the tinted glass. Looking back was a slight, balding man with thick glasses who, in spite of the best suiting wool and the most expensive tailoring, looked rumpled, with an odd gap between his coat collar and the side of his neck.

Unlike his brother Ernst, Schopfer Chemical's chief executive officer, Robert bore no resemblance to the portrait of their father hanging on the far wall. He always avoided looking at the picture. The painter had done a too-good job capturing the old man's hard eyes always looking down on him with disapproval, just as they had when Bobby and Ernst were small boys, or large boys, or young men, or middle-aged men. Hans had ruled with an iron fist until he was eighty-two, when he grudgingly surrendered nominal control to his sons.

Bobby was content with the title he and his brother agreed on, Senior Vice President, which put him in charge of anything that would be hard to screw up— employee relations, pensions, medical benefits, and art and advertising. All of these areas were headed by competent managers who required little supervision. So Robert and Zelda busied themselves with charity, focused on the city's underprivileged.

Today Bobby dreaded a meeting his brother had called with Joe Graber, the corporation's recently-appointed president. Ernie had made it clear that Bobby's attendance was mandatory. The agenda was important. Moreover, Graber was a dynamic, animated executive around whom Bobby felt insecure. Graber had been Ernst's choice for president.

He and his brother together held almost forty percent of the outstanding shares, more than enough to call the shots, and Bobby always voted as Ernst directed.

After years of steady, profitable growth, Schopfer Chemical had been struggling the last few years. Revenue continued to climb but profits had shrunk. Long term debt and interest payments had risen sharply. Part of the problem lay with the sluggish national economy, but more troublesome had been the diversification plan Ernst had pushed through the board.

When he entered the business, Ernst had chafed under the old man's steely will and what he regarded as his father's outdated ideas. He had arrived on the Schoper Chemical scene full of enthusiasm and the latest management ideas he had learned at Harvard Business School, but Hans brushed them aside. His father had been phenomenally successful and the ideas Ernst found stifling Hans saw as conservative and intelligent, building on the internal technical strengths of the company with expansion financed from current profits. Hans's paternalistic treatment of his employees—good salaries, a generous pension plan, and job security with a solid company—produced feverish, Japanese-style loyalty.

When Ernst got hold of the reins of power, he sought to make up for lost time by buying small companies in fields foreign to the company's expertise. Many of these hastily-acquired firms turned out to be duds. Ernst, initially energized by the heady flush of being in control, able to make decisions that his minions were required to execute, becoming comfortable with the glib language of modern corporate finance—acquisition of technology, diversification, synergies—had been gradually deflated by the unhealthy balance sheets and meager profits from the purchased firms. The details of this bad news were buried in annual statements, but he couldn't hide the fact that total profit margins for the corporation had slipped since the days when Hans ran the show.

Like a reckless, desperate gambler, Ernst had plunged on, oblivious to his father's glowering image and dismissing the penetrating questions, embarrassed throat clearing, and creaking chairs of nervous, fidgety stockholders at the annual meetings. Ernst doubled his bets, diving into high risk fields recommended by his confident VP of Research, Dr. Bellington, and his close ally on the board, Joe Graber. Resistance from the board of directors was easily blown past now that he and Graber had managed to push into retirement the last three strong men left over from his father's day and replace them with his own handpicked candidates.

Once they saw the way the wind was blowing, the rest of the board fell into step. They were encouraged to adapt to the desirable attribute of modern business, flexibility. Of course, it would have been rude to point out that flexible, pliable, and malleable were akin. Pliable and malleable men were tolerable when a strong leader shaped, inspired, and directed them, but they were incapable of decisive action on their own. When the leader misdirected, that "flexibility" meant agreeing with his mistakes. Worse, they tried to rescue popular programs that had been mismanaged beyond redemption.

They endorsed optimistic reports on the potential of Ernst's and Graber's programs, while dismissing present problems. Dr. Bellington assured the directors and officers that his brilliant research program was on the verge of producing great advances that would result in new products that would find big markets. Early in Ernst's reign, some of the directors offered a few words of constructive criticism, but they were met by carefully-crafted but unmistakable rebukes. Good money was thrown after bad, as the company spent more and more profligately, hoping for serendipitous hits which would yield winners.

Potential products were snatched from Research before being thoroughly proven and trumpeted at the next board meeting. Short cuts were taken in production processes, test marketing, safety, and health studies to race potentially saleable products to customers. In an industry where the failure rate for new product developments was about eighty percent—even after rigorous research and extensive market testing—Schopfer Chemical was neglecting to properly pre-test new products, pushing its failure rate even higher. The flow of funds to the marketing and production of failures was suffocating the company's core business.

The Research Department, instead of conducting long-range research, found itself occupied with the rushed, uncontrolled frenzy to find quick solutions.

Short-term thinking began to infect Schopfer Chemical. Directors voted themselves larger blocks of stock options, bigger pensions, and deferred bonuses. Employee morale sank as managers found their budgets shrinking and bonuses reduced, even though their own operations were performing well.

Bobby Schopfer was unable to fathom why, but the unexpressed frustration and pessimism of others had managed, by osmosis, to creep into his cushioned cell. He felt a wave of dread when the connecting door to his brother's office swung open and Ernst and Joe Graber bustled into the room. Ernst grimaced and sat himself down like a sack.

Ernst had always been Bobby's big brother, in fact and in spirit. They enjoyed their roles and there was genuine affection between them. But to be the object or giver of true affection is so rare that it should be accepted on faith. Its motives or degree of perfection should not be subjected to examination, except by intellectual fools.

Ernst sighed and began the meeting. "Bobby, Joe is putting together a plan to present at the next management committee meeting and I would like him to brief you on it and get your comments, which I'm sure he'll want to incorporate. Now, there are some parts to this which may be distasteful to you, as they certainly were to me. However, these are the facts of economic life now and Joe, coming back from Europe, has the advantage of a more objective outside view of our organization and.... Oh hell, I'm getting in the way, Joe. Why don't you just outline your program?"

Bobby leaned back in his chair and swiveled slightly to the side so that he did not have to look directly at the pair opposite him, but he swerved too far and he found himself staring into the eyes of his father's portrait. He swung back in the other direction and prepared to be addressed, on a matter of obvious importance, by a man who made him nervous.

Graber reviewed the state of the economy and then cast Schopfer against this background. Bobby heard all of this indistinctly, until a key line broke through his controlled agitation. "My conclusion is that Schopfer Chemical is performing too poorly to be explicable on the basis of the national economy. Even more pertinent, its position in the chemical industry is actually in decline. The reasons must be found internally."

Startled, Bobby wheeled and blinked directly at Graber. Graber paused, giving him a chance to speak. When he did not, he continued. "Now when conclusions such as this one are made, the normal and facile thing to do is to assume that management needs revamping and the directors are sacrificed. But, by God, I don't believe that's true for Schopfer. I've only been associated briefly with some of the directors, but I have found them to be an inspiring and outstanding group!"

Bobby wanted to speak, but he didn't know what Graber was driving at. He mildly said, "Yes, interesting. Go on, please."

Joe took a breath. "I believe the problem lies in the way the company philosophy evolved under your father. Now I know he was a remarkable man and his achievements were tremendous. However, times change and what worked well for him may not be consistent with the best interests of today's large corporation. The innate generosity and Christian values of the fine old gentleman led to a paternalistic treatment of employees which was fine and good when he knew virtually everyone, before some of our employees belonged to powerful unions, and workers still had pride in their jobs.

"Today, things are different. Workers are motivated mostly by fear for their own security. This motivation is lacking at Schopfer. Every employee knows that it is virtually impossible to fire someone with seniority. In their view, the company is very secure financially."

Ernst sat quietly, puffing deliberately on a cigar. He had never been permitted to smoke in his father's presence and for a period of time no smoking had been allowed in the offices. Now he indulged in an occasional, large, and rank stogie, the primary purposes of which were to:

1. Make him look executive-like.

2. Give him something to do with his hands when nervous.

3. Allow him to stall and think before replying, by hesitating for a puff.

Number two was in operation now. Ernst surreptitiously studied Bobby's face for his reaction as Graber's words became more and more pointed. He knew Bobby would be upset, at least at first, and that he would have to work on him to enlist his necessary support. He wanted to determine the depth of his negative reaction, so that he could plan his coming campaign.

"In short," Graber continued, "many of the senior employees have become fat cats and no longer pull their load. This has necessitated the hiring of additional employees. The inflated staff has become the main contributor to our present problems."

Joe paused, caught Bobby face to face, and very deliberately, with great emphasis said, "I believe a staff reduction of ten to fifteen percent is required to return Schopfer to a competitive position."

Bobby jerked his chair upright and his eyebrows arched. He stared at Ernie in disbelief, tilting his head like a dog whose master has suddenly made an unfamiliar sound. "You really don't plan to fire a lot of employees, do you?"

Ernie put on his best soothing tone. "Bobby, I know that Joe's conclusion sounds harsh and is completely out of character for the company, but it's also out of character for our profits to be declining. We have got to remember that our first duty as directors of a public corporation is to protect our stockholders."

Bobby sputtered. "We can't just start firing faithful employees! Why... It just...."

Graber waited a respectful moment, then said, "Mr. Schopfer, let me explain that when I say a ten to fifteen percent reduction, it really does not mean firing that many people. Much of it can be accomplished by a hiring freeze and attrition. Our normal attrition rate is eight percent per year from deaths, retirements, and people leaving for other jobs."

Bobby puffed a sigh of relief. "So that means you're just proposing a halt to hiring until our staff comes in line, right?"

"I'm afraid not, Mr. Schopfer. Some can be accomplished that way. However, the attrition rate is down right now because of the surplus labor market. Secondly, in all honesty, there has to be some shock treatment applied to the 'coasting' senior employees. Some of them are the real cause of our overstaffing. If they read this just as a freeze, or even as a layoff on the usual basis of seniority, they would continue smugly on their way.

"Some senior employees have to go. Of course, selection will have to be considered very carefully in order to be just and to achieve maximum effect with minimum pain, as is the correct moral approach.

"I further propose that we tackle this campaign from a positive view of rallying the company to make an energetic new beginning, rather than from a defeatist attitude. I believe all good employees will understand and be ready to join in the fight to make Schopfer strong again."

Bobby turned to his brother, a note of pleading in his voice, "Ernie, do you really believe this is necessary? Couldn't we ride it out? The two of us could keep the stockholders in line for another year or so. The economy is bound to pick up in that time. Besides, we already have the Bridesburg plant problem on our plate."

Ernst cleared his throat. "I wish we could, but there are rumblings about a minority stockholders revolt. Just as Joe noted, when things go badly, the first instinct is to sacrifice the directors, who are our friends. We probably could hold out, but it would get very messy and I'm sure you don't want that. Besides you have to take the view of what is best for the most people." He examined the end of his cigar, then took another puff.

"Remember, by making the company solid you are really protecting the interest and security of ninety percent of the employees who are working hard. In addition, when we displace some of the slackers, we intend to bring in some fine young blacks and females as replacements. I know this has always been a great concern of yours, and I would like you to take charge of this aspect of the program. As for the Bridesburg plant problem, I'm handling that personally, so you don't have to get involved."

Ernst was satisfied he'd finessed the situation by first giving Bobby a glimpse of the unthinkable, where he might be under fire in public, and then providing him with a noble rationale to escape it.

Bobby had no stomach or the skills to manage the growing health problems at Bridesburg. He would gladly allow Ernst to shield him from any corporate unpleasantness that might develop there. The chance to brag about hiring minority and disadvantaged people appealed to his social self-image. Bobby's resistance crumbled under Ernst's well-constructed assault. Ernst knew it would rise again in the future, but he also knew his brother well—Bobby's whining would diminish in intensity and he would be able to control it.

Ernst took little pleasure in this victory, as necessary as it was. He did not like the program any more than did Bobby, and there was no joy in successfully manipulating his brother. In fact, he felt a sense of failure. He had always prided himself on his older-brother role, keeping Bobby content in his cocoon, protected from the ugliness of life. Now he had to drag him through some of the muck. He knew from a lifetime of experience that Bobby's stomach would be churning just as, when their father scolded them as children for some trivial infraction of his moral code, Bobby would develop a wicked stomach ache. This time, Bobby would be ill for several days.

Ernst sighed to himself—no triumph. The feeling was more like having a good bowel movement after a protracted period of constipation, and stunk about the same.

Bobby placed a hand over his mid-section and said softly, "Give me some time to think about this."

"Sure, sure." Ernst and Graber rose, collecting their papers. "But we're on a tight time schedule. We plan to lay this program out at the next management committee meeting."

As they headed out the door, Ernst turned and said, "It'll all work out, Bobby. I'll see to it."

Bobby stood and resumed pacing around his office. He paused and forced himself to study his father's portrait, and paused again to stare out the window, northward on the Delaware River to the company's Bridesburg plant. He thought maybe if he went home he could keep the cramps in his stomach from getting worse.

Chapter Four

The Road Taken

On Monday morning after the pool party, Harry's phone rang steadily with congratulatory calls from well-wishers—sincere and otherwise. The news had spread with amazing speed. The last call of the morning had brought yet another surprise. Ernst invited him to attend a special meeting of the management committee on Tuesday, and for lunch on Friday. It was unusual for assistant VPs to attend these meetings, but Ernst explained that this was to be an exceptional session.

He apologized to Harry for the month's delay in moving into his new office until Ben Jensen retired. Harry joked that he'd be happy to have an office in the boiler room, as long as he had the job responsibilities and title. As usual, neither mentioned money, relatively low on the list of motivators for senior executives after power, influence, and control. Money was more of a measuring stick for progress or slippage in the pecking order; a way of keeping score.

Shortly after Ernst's phone call, there was a rap on the door and Charley Winston's silver hair and ruddy complexion peered around the edge. "Got a minute to talk with a peon?"

Harry grinned. "You're down to fifty-five seconds now."

Charley entered, sat opposite Harry, stretched out his legs and sighed. "All that dancing, food, and good booze at your house nearly did me in. Agnes was giving me hell all the way home."

Harry noticed that Charley's high color was more pronounced than usual. "You'd better watch your blood pressure, you old bastard. You still act like the hotshot young field salesman."

Harry felt a genuine affection for Charley, an open and charismatic mentor who'd taught him so much and helped Harry avoid some early missteps when he first came in to the home office. Harry had been promoted from an outside district field sales manager to a position working inside. Charley had been the closest thing to a friend and confidante at Schopfer.

"Listen, Charley, I was totally taken by surprise when Bobby—" Charley waved his hand to cut him off.

"Harry, I couldn't say the things I wanted to at the party, but I'm going to say them now. You are the best damn executive I have ever seen, and I have had contact with a lot of the big ones." Harry squirmed and opened his mouth to speak, but Charley plowed on.

"You just sit there and listen, because I'm only going to do this once. So far, you have operated on pure ability and hard work, but from now on those things are going to be of less value to you. You are going to have to develop political allies. In fact, they will be more important to you now than pure ability. Consult with them, even when you know the right answer. Listen when they talk. Sit on your tongue, which can be too fast. Socialize with them—even at the expense of your old friends."

Charley waited until Harry's gaze met his before continuing. "I mean that last item, you only owe loyalty to your family and those above you. Become more cautious and introspective. Harry, you have got a fine chance to go all the way. You could be president or chairman, which would be a damn fine thing for you and all of the people who work here. This outfit needs really competent people in the higher ranks.

"I only hope Schopfer is strong enough to survive the present crew. You're the type of man who could make it vibrant again, the way it was when the old man was around. Business decisions were made on the basis of technology and marketing, not by MBA financial nerds! End of speech. Now let's go out for lunch and I'll buy the beers."

"Thanks, Charley." Harry said. "You're on for the beers and I'll want a stein as a kickback, as I'll be recommending you for new assignments in the future."

Harry's intercom buzzed and his secretary announced, "Mr. Robert Schopfer wants to know if you are free to lunch with him today." Harry looked at Charley, who gave him a thumbs up and shrugged. Harry chuckled, and replied, "Yes I'm free."

As Charley headed for the door, he said, "You didn't have to start so soon. Maybe Friday?"

"I'm having lunch with Ernst."

"Jesus, you are fast."

"I'm holding Wednesday for you, okay?"

"Okay, boss!"

Lunch at the Barclay Hotel was a first for Harry. Also new was the luxurious service. They had been driven the few blocks from the Schopfer Building to the hotel in Bobby's chauffeured Chrysler Imperial. The enormous, stately trees in toney Rittenhouse Square were in early leaf, shading an odd melange of wealthy matrons, porters, and pampered purebred dogs. Scruffy hippies lounged on the grass. Men in bowties, short sleeve white shirts, and folded lightweight suitcoats, sat on the benches enjoying the fine weather.

The Barclay doorman opened the car door with a "Good day, Mr. Schopfer."

"Good day, George."

Bobby, carrying himself with regal poise that Harry had never seen, led the way to the dining room. Harry observed the difference it makes when a person knows that other people know he is important.

"Michael, a quiet table please," Bobby instructed the maitré d'hotel. "I'd like to introduce my personal friend, Mr. Harry Schoen. I'm sure he'll always receive your courteous attention."

"Yes, of course, Mr. Schopfer." The maitre d' gave Harry a crisp, appraising smile and a split-second once-over. "Mr. Schoen."

"Michael."

The talk in the car had been small and continued through the excellent luncheon. Bobby neither smoked nor drank and Harry refrained. One of his skills was being attuned to people and astutely reading their attitudes, choices, tones, and words to gain their trust.

With lunch nearly over, and nothing of substance having been discussed, he glanced over the top of his coffee cup and ventured, "Something troubling you, Robert?"

"Yes. Yes there is Harry, and I don't know how to bridge the subject."

"Well, why not just state the problem and make your comments on the basis that anything you say is subject to withdrawal, reconsideration, and polishing before being regarded as final. It's a good technique for getting started on sticky wickets."

"All right, I'll use your ploy." Bobby paused, collecting himself before continuing. "Harry, the management committee meeting tomorrow is going to be . . . extraordinary, a radical proposal for change in the, um, philosophy of the company. Ernie and Mr. Graber are in favor of it and they believe that it is necessary. I'm not sure, not sure at all...."

Harry sat frozen in rapt attention as Bobby stumbled on, but kept his thoughts to himself.

"I would like you to listen carefully, say nothing, but go home and ponder the plan carefully, then give me your thoughts on it in the morning. Will you do that for me?"

Harry's curiosity was inflamed, but he knew better than to drill for details. He was disturbed that he was being drawn outside the realm of "strictly business," and into that of confidante, pet, or some other less savory role. With Charley's advice fresh in his mind—to tend to political allies—he recognized that Robert would normally be a tremendous ally, but a poor one in any disagreement with his brother and

Joe Graber. On the other hand, considering Bobby had been the engine of Harry's rise, he could not refuse. He was glad he'd have time to weigh the issue.

"All right, Robert. If you wish."

Bobby seemed relieved. "Thank you, Harry. Before you react to the plan, you should be aware of the health problems at the Bridesburg plant."

"I've heard rumors, but I really don't know anything."

Robert avoided Harry's eyes. "Unfortunately, there are problems emerging with lung cancers. I can't go into detail, but I'm deeply concerned that the health issue will be a big problem for employee morale and that layering on this new business plan will compound the situation."

"I'll do my best for you."

Back at his desk, Harry's secretary buzzed him. "Mr. Winston's office on line two."

"Hello, Charley."

Marie's voice responded: "Congratulations, Harry. I just needed to call," explaining why she was violating their strict rule of avoiding unnecessary contact at work.

"Thanks, Marie." He raised his voice a notch, to business-as-usual. "Did you ask Charley if it was all right to change our late meeting from Thursday to today?"

"He said he can make it."

"Good. I'll stop by and pick him up."

Harry called Nancy but she was out. "She went to the club to play golf with Mr. and Mrs. Warden," Marcy reported.

"Will you leave the message that I won't be home for dinner. In fact, I'll probably be late. My new boss wants to have dinner and discuss plans."

"Okay Mistah Schoen. And thank you for the goodies on Saturday," she added in a conspiratorial whisper.

Old John Warden must be getting soft, Harry mused. He always complained about women on the golf course and now he was playing a round with two of them.

———

Later that night, Harry lay between the clean white sheets, his body cool and refreshed by a shower. He recalled Ben Franklin's letter to a young friend advising him to choose a mistress who was older rather than younger: Women wrinkled from the top down, and older women didn't yell, didn't tell, didn't swell, and were grateful as hell.

He was glad Marie had been able to see him tonight instead of waiting until Thursday. He felt great. A fine candlelight dinner at the Emperor, good alcohol, and now a sturdy erection as he waited for Marie. Damn, he thought, this is the best thing that's happened to me.

He felt a small twinge of guilt over the hypocrisy of his behavior versus what he'd taught his children about morals and ethics. But he had his rationalizations: their relationship was less an affair than a love discovered late in life. And it was a release that helped him hold his family together, for the benefit of the children. It was less painful than the alternative, divorce.

He enjoyed making Marie happy and often outdid himself with thoughtful gestures. The price of the relationship was borne equally by Harry and Marie, consisting of guilt and longing. Harry's need for intimacy and emotional release was growing.

Marie finally entered the room in her kimono. She let it fall open as she stood in the soft glow of the hall light. She removed the Spanish comb holding her gray-streaked hair, turning slightly as she picked up her brush from the dresser and gave her hair a few expert pulls.

All the lovely parts were peeking out of her kimono. He felt a delicious ache coming on. She switched on the radio to some soft music, sat on the edge of the bed with her back to him and lit a cigarette.

She's playing me like a fish on a line, he thought. He closed his eyes and opened his mouth slightly. He took a few slow deep breaths. "Harry?" No answer. A little louder, "Harry?" He suddenly dove across the bed and caught her in his arms.

"That'll teach you a lesson." He kissed her, bit her earlobe, her neck, and nuzzled his head below her chin.

She chuckled and pulled away, stood up and slipped the kimono off while he appraised her shadowy body. She slipped beneath the sheets and snuggled against his arm. "Oh darling, what a lovely way to end a lovely evening." She reached across his belly.

"Damn it lady, please-a no squeeze-a da banana."

"It's all right. I'm going to eat it here."

"You sweet lover you. I'm trying to go slow, and you make me feel like taking you."

"Hmmm sounds delightful. But let's stretch it out."

"I wish I could, in more ways than one."

"Oh darling you fill me and...um, that feels good." His head was now beneath the sheet.

"You have beautiful breasts and so convenient— one on each side".

"I love it when you caress them."

He lightly stroked the inside of her thigh. As his head moved down her body, the sheet rippled like snow drifts. Marie, her eyes nearly closed, dropped her head on the pillow, arched her back, and pulled his mouth against her as she thrust her body into it. His arms looped under her legs up her sides and his fingers stroked her breasts while his tongue darted between her legs. Marie chewed on her lower lip. Her tongue licked her upper lip.

"Omm, omm, omm, OMM! Damn it, give it to me!"

He jumped to comply.

All gentleness was discarded as they thrust against one another. He grabbed Marie's buttocks and pulled her to him as he kneeled with her legs over his shoulders. Harry began to sway and moan softly as they bounced in rhythm.

"Come on, lover, get it all. Let my joy juice fly into your sweet pussy."

She convulsed as his body shuddered and the stream of life flowed into her.

They lay, still joined but not as deeply, on their

sides. Harry, now all gentleness with eyes moist with emotion, kissed her forehead, eyelids, and lips. He whispered in her ear, "So much for the foreplay. Now let's make love." She giggled. "It feels great when I'm in you and you giggle."

"It's too bad that sex is the most fun you can have without laughing."

"I'll get a tank of laughing gas or try to catch you when you have a coughing spell. Maybe that was the 'Appeal of Camille?'"

"You've got ten minutes fellow, and then I want a repeat and you're going to keep doing it over until you get it right." She tickled his ribs.

Harry lit a cigarette. The bright flame blinded him briefly. He placed the cigarette between her lips. He thought it was wonderful that, unlike other animals, humans can both blow and suck.

"Babs is getting married soon and Nancy and I are further apart than ever. Also, I suspect that shortly I'll be earning one hell of a lot of money."

"Let's not go into that again."

"Now wait. I have been living with this for a while, and I don't like treating you this way, but why not this fall? You could quit work and I could start a divorce. I'll be able to provide a generous settlement for Nancy and we could have a wonderful life together."

Marie responded with an edge in her voice. "Number one: I'm too old for you." He started to protest, but she placed her hand over his lips. He kissed her fingers. "Seven years is a lot—maybe not right now, but in another ten years it will be, and I have too much pride to rely on a ring for protection. I always have the lights dim so you can't see my cellulite and spider veins. When I'm old, you'll be looking at all those tight little asses around the office."

She pulled away as he tried to kiss her.

"Not until I finish lover. Number two: it would hurt your relationship with your children. I know they're close to being on their own, but it would only be natural for them to resent the fact that you disturbed their cozy little worlds.

"Number three: I would not like to be responsible for having any adverse effect on your career. You're moving fast, the Schopfers are blue noses, and your career is very important to you, and also to me. I take great pride in your accomplishments.

"Number four: it's sweet of you to want to marry me. God, how I wish we had met years ago! But I'm a big girl. I can stand being your mistress rather than your wife. I appreciate that you're trying to make an honest woman of me, but it isn't necessary. Please be positive that your offer is not to soothe your own guilty feelings. I love being your lover.

"And last but not least, as they say," she paused and her voice went soft, "I think you still have feelings for Nancy."

Harry stroked her hair. "You know the old saw says that whenever two people are in bed, there are really four; the two present and the others that they wish were there. But I can assure you that you're the only female present and my thoughts are only for you."

Marie turned away from Harry's gaze. "I never think of any man I ever had prior to you. I'd only had a few and never with the intensity of passion I experience with you. I can't explain it, but I go wild with you. I'm like a nymphomaniac. I enjoy the dirty talk and rough sex, but afterwards I feel like a naughty little girl who has played doctor with the little boy next door."

"Whatever you're doing, keep doing it," he said. "I need you badly. All day long I have to wear a suit of armor and play Dead Pan Poker and then go home to a cold house, not a home, where I mustn't wrinkle the upholstery.

"One item I take exception to is the accusation of looking at all those tight little asses. Well, let's exclude looking. When I fail to notice attractive women, put me in a hole and throw dirt on me. But as for doing more, no way. Look, you know that I know that sex is available all over the place, but love is fucking rare."

Marie gave him a sad smile, "Being with you is wonderful but it can't last. Please stop telling me I'm the only one for you. Otherwise, when you stop telling me, I'll know what you're saying."

Chapter Five

A Bend in the Road

T he newly appointed Assistant VP of Marketing, Harry Schoen, entered the boardroom in the company of his predecessor, Jack Boswelth, the newly crowned VP of Marketing. Harry had been in the room before, but only when summoned to make a presentation and then dismissed as a completed agenda item.

The management committee members drifted into the room in ones and twos with hearty greetings and a great deal of smiling, bordering on joviality. Harry knew this joviality was false, a thin tissue papering over the jealousies and struggles that attended their courtier positions about the throne. It was akin to a meeting of politicians who all support the party, but all want to be the nominee or enjoy the favor of the one person who will be able to help them in the future.

"Well, here's where I leave you Harry," Boswelth said. "You can take a seat in the 'bullpen' side there." He motioned to a row of seats. "After thirty-eight years, and less than two years to go until retirement, I finally get to sit with the big boys."

Boswelth strolled over to the large oval walnut

table surrounded by high-backed leather swivel chairs. The members greeted Boswelth with handshakes, congratulating him on joining the management group. Boswelth was someone for whom the good wishes might actually be sincere—he had no future. He was just an interim caretaker of the VP of Marketing position. He posed no threat to their plans or plots.

Boswelth had done an excellent job of being the hale-fellow-well-met. He was an expert fence-sitter. Harry calculated that Boswelth's indecisiveness would be both irritating and useful. It would be irritating to have to pretend that Boswelth was his boss and useful because he'd have two years to learn the job and worm his way into actual control, so he would be a strong, experienced candidate when Boswelth retired. Harry had plenty of self-confidence, but he also learned from his bosses, even when it was what not to do. He studied them, storing the wheat and discarding the chaff.

The far door to the room opened and Bobby, Ernst, and Graber entered as a group. The conversation in the room died rapidly as everyone took their seats. Ernst sat at the head of the table, flanked by Bobby and Graber, and in place of a gavel, cleared his throat.

"First, I would like to welcome our new VP and Assistant VP of Marketing." A round of smiles and nods were directed at Boswelth and Harry.

"Gentlemen, this is a key meeting, a turning point in the history of Schopfer Chemical. It marks a time of spirited new growth and development, and overdue modernization and trimming of fat.

"Gentlemen, this company collectively, and all our employees individually, are going to get in fighting trim. Now, this will not be accomplished without some pain." Ernst paused and gave the assemblage a quick sweep, perhaps gauging first reactions.

"Now to the main order today—the only order of business. When you allow yourself to become soft it is difficult to become fit again. However, I am sure that with your enthusiastic and able support, the strong base of the company, the loyalty of the great bulk of our employees, and adherence to the plan that Joe has designed so masterfully, this company will re-emerge as a leader in the chemical industry. This plan will yield greater security and growth opportunities for our employees, high earnings for our stockholders, and funds for expansion. Joe, your ball."

Ernst leaned back and began to unwrap a cigar as Graber got to his feet and placed poster-sized cards on an easel at the side of the table. The board members stirred slightly as they swiveled their chairs and prepared to pretend to take notes.

"Gentlemen, first I would like to provide you with a little background. I am sure much of this will be familiar to you, but it will serve as useful reference material for what will come.

"Chart I: A graph of our profits as a percent of total sales over the last twenty years. Note that these lines rise, up until about five or six years ago. Note that while sales continued to rise, our profits began to fall.

"Now, we are all aware of the generally unfavorable economic trends during that period and it would be convenient to view the decline in that light, expecting things to improve as the national economy does. But what if that is not the whole story? What if something basic is wrong at Schopfer that keeps us from responding when the economy changes?"

Graber paused, surveying the faces.

"How could we determine such a thing? Well let's see what chart two tells us. First, let's look at the graph of Schopfer Chemical and the other fourteen largest chemical companies' relative standing on percent profit. Note that ten years ago we were number two, second only to DuPont, and last year we were number nine! And the latest readings are still sinking! I don't think we can blame this fact on the state of the national economy."

"I have a comment on that item, Joe," a voice softly interrupted. He was an old-timer up from the ranks, an engineer who had progressed through virtually every line supervision position in production to become the VP in charge of production. As a supervisor responsible for concrete results, he had a low tolerance for staff presentations based upon reinterpretations of "carefully selected" historical data and opinions. His own career had been one massive series of real problems, which had honed his analytical mind to a fine edge. His was the natural aversion of the medieval baron who had just returned from battling the invaders at the border, exacting taxes from the peasants, and preventing revolt, only to find a courtier held a more exalted position with the king.

The courtiers, staff, in modern parlance, dealt in subjective matters or pleasantries, such as, "Would the king prefer to wench or hunt?" or in matters of opinion which were qualitative. The advertising manager says sales of the item are down, but just think how bad it might have been without our advertising.

"Yes, Mr. Farnum?" Graber shifted his weight to one foot, awaiting the question, hoping it would be one from the list of potential items for which he had carefully developed pat answers.

"That graph showing reduced profits on higher sales was not totally caused by our increased plant investments, but more from assets gained via our acquisition program. It strikes me that if they were factored out, our profits would still look good."

Ouch! Harry thought. Farnum had indirectly blamed Ernst's acquisition program. The medieval baron's weapons, the battle axe and the mace, which Mr. Farnum wielded so effectively to get new chemical plants completed on time and within budget, were never suitable for the intrigues of boardroom/court. Weapons of choice were stiletto and rapier—the stiletto to be used in the dark from behind, and the rapier to make small shallow slashes to the front. It was not necessary to slay your opponent by "the death of a thousand cuts" or thrusting through his heart like Cyrano De Bergerac. A few small bleeding cuts proved that he was not invincible and the circling sharks were ready to finish him off.

"Don," Ernst interrupted with a note of deliberate irritation, "you have a valid point but it is not the major parameter. Now let's get on with the presentation."

Farnum's eyes narrowed as he scribbled a note on the pad in front of him.

Graber resumed, now with the guarantee of a docile audience. Chart after chart was silently acknowledged by nodding heads, until at last Graber brought out his key point.

"In short, gentlemen, we are a business that has gotten out of shape. Our research takes too long, our marketing targets are too vague, our salesmanship is too casual, our production too costly, our credit policies too lenient. All of these factors add up to one word: INEFFICIENT.

"How did this situation arise? Likely through success and growth, while attempting to continue doing business in the same manner which served us so well when we were smaller. These old methods allowed us to increase sales, but growth, without applying modern financial control methods, resulted in inefficiencies. Combined with this, the paternalistic character of our organization has led to overstaffing. Our reluctance to fire under-performing employees forced managers to add personnel to compensate for those who were not effective."

Harry studied his cufflinks. Here goes old Hans's loyalty-to-employees philosophy out the window!

"The prescription is obvious, although the final details have not yet been selected. An essential feature of the program will involve M.B.O. I'm sure that most of you are familiar with the term and have read articles on the subject, but basically Management By Objectives is a format for achieving corporate goals. This starts at the top of our organization and trickles down to the lower levels, so that each person has goals which are consistent with those of the entire company. In effect, it is a method of achieving corporate coordination so that all the oars are pulling in the same direction. Copies of a book explaining the technique are available for your consideration."

Ernst cleared his throat. "Excuse me for a moment, Joe. I would like to emphasize the importance of the book, which may be found on Miss Hill's desk. I have studied this technique and discussed it in great detail with Joe and business consultants from the Harvard Business School, and I am most enthusiastic about its potential for Schopfer. I am requesting that you study this book closely, as it will be the main topic of an additional meeting in approximately two weeks."

Harry smiled, but not with pleasure. He knew the translation for Ernst's helpful suggestion: I have decided that this is what you're going to do, so read the book because I'm going to ask questions. Harry was familiar with MBO and had used it to build his department's reputation for efficiency. MBO theory had been established by Harvard's Peter Drucker, whose many books and followers had made him into a legend. But MBO had its detractors. At firms that had tried and abandoned the program, the standard joke was that it had been dreamed up by the professor's mother and was thus referred to as "The Mother Drucker MBO Plan."

Graber ploughed on.

"We are going to re-emphasize our mission while reaffirming our responsibility to society and to the environment. These points are not new, having originated with Mr. Hans Schopfer, and have been continued by Robert and Ernst.

"However, one definition of time is change, and a great deal of time and change has taken place since our founding. Schopfer Chemical is similar to a champion fighter who has slackened off and suddenly discovers that he is lying on the canvas. The really great ones get up and fight back and win!" Graber made a clumsy attempt at punching the air with his right fist.

"And that is what Schopfer is going to do. We are not going to degenerate into a purveyor of commodity goods at commodity prices. Lord knows there are enough of them already in the chemical industry. We are going to be champions again, by following this game plan."

Harry understood why, although it was a principal cause of the problem, Graber ignored Ernst's disastrous business diversification program. It would have been political suicide to point out that the Emperor had no clothes. But he accepted the notion that Graber's program might produce additional profits to tide the company over and soothe the stockholders, until the hemorrhaging could be staunched.

Graber next outlined the program, which included trimming fat, reducing pollution, and boosting minority hiring. The language he used for the last one was a bit ham-handed, Harry thought, and the implementation sounded decidedly non-MBO.

"We are going to hire disadvantaged, unqualified people and then pay for their education and training. We are going to give them preference in promotions and they will have to be proven to be disqualified, rather than to be the best qualified. There will be more minority employees hired and they will be promoted more rapidly than others, and managers will do all in their power to aid them."

Harry glanced at Bobby who, rather than listening attentively to Graber, was doodling. Harry was puzzled. Graber was getting down the list and so far it sounded like an A-1 talk to encourage financial analysts, stock holders, social planners and government. The last item should have fit right into Bobby and Zelda's social/philanthropic vein. It would be hell for the managers to implement, but should have aroused Bobby's enthusiasm.

Graber continued, "In order to achieve these goals, some sacrifices are going to be needed. To begin reshaping our profit statement and convincing employees that we're serious, I am recommending a highly unusual and distasteful step for Schopfer." Every head—except Bobby's—snapped to attention. All the bored chair squirming, pen twirling, thumb rubbing, and foot shifting suddenly ceased.

Graber seemed to gulp for air. "At Ernst's request, I have studied this organization from the time of my recall from overseas and have been greatly impressed with the executive ability of the gentlemen I have had contact with. But I am also aware of the common reaction of stockholders when a company's profits decline. Gentlemen, that reaction is to change the management. I personally disagree with that tactic for Schopfer, but I find that we have become paternalistic."

Graber's voice seemed to rise a few notes up the scale as he announced, "I have personally recommended a reduction in work force across the board, of ten to fifteen percent."

The stunned silence was broken only by a collective gasp that seemed to have escaped Graber's notice.

"This is to be partially accomplished by a hiring freeze, and natural attrition via retirements, deaths, and normal departures, but I have deliberately proposed the systematic identification and termination of laggards, without regard to seniority. I have made the latter proposal on a deliberate basis in order to shake some of the lethargic, civil-service-like attitudes out of our workforce and make it clear that our employees must continuously earn the right to be members of this organization."

Harry winced. This could become a witch hunt, he thought, and sunder the bonds with the employees that Hans had so carefully cultivated.

"Gentlemen, I dislike this step, but I firmly believe that strong medicine is needed in order to be fair to the other ninety percent of our loyal employees. To this end I strongly recommend that a positive program, which I call 'BOB', or 'Boost Our Business', be adopted. Note that I place emphasis on the words 'positive' and 'our'. Thank you for your attention and consideration of this effort."

A storm of throat clearing followed.

After the usual praise of a chairman for his chosen president, Ernst lied magnificently. "Gentlemen, Bobby and I have not yet fully endorsed the last point of Joe's program. However, I am inclined to reluctantly agree. When you've had time to reflect, I'm available to hear your thoughts, comments, and advice. Needless to say, this is all highly confidential. Meeting adjourned."

Ernst, Bobby, and Graber rose and departed silently through the rear door. The managers sat in stunned silence for a long moment, then rose and departed quietly, their faces as blank as dinner plates, although Harry knew that every one couldn't wait to discuss it with their trusted allies.

Harry stopped at the desk and mechanically picked up a copy of the MBO book, and wandered off toward the elevator with Jack Boswelth.

"We sure as hell picked great times to get promoted, Harry. What do you think?"

"I think I'm going to say nothing until I do a lot of thinking."

"I'll bet five-to-one that Ernst has already decided in favor of it, and that he just wants to take on dissenters on a one-to-one basis to prevent any organized resistance. I think I'll reflect for a day, and then go pledge my confidence in his judgment, and express sympathy for his responsibility."

Harry grinned conspiratorially. "Jack, I think I can learn a great deal from you."

Chapter Six

Sauce for the Goose and Gosling

John Warden swung his black Buick into the sweeping driveway, and guided it to a halt in front of the porticoed entrance with its glistening white columns. He felt a warm glow of self-satisfaction as he surveyed the gracious white house, with its black shutters and palladian panels of glass atop the tall windows.

One entire wing was devoted to housing John's extensive library and his wife Anne's grand piano, which she played frequently and rather well thanks to several years of study at the Curtis Institute of Music.

The other wing housed a solarium with many plants and a bar. French doors opened to a brick patio, with steps leading to a tennis court. A side door from the kitchen permitted breakfast service. A path led through the garden to a heated swimming pool and cabana.

The house and grounds surpassed those of the surrounding properties, which gave John Warden great pleasure, even though he had married every last cent. He happily anticipated the death that would place his father-in-law's entire, and much larger estate, in his grip, replete with a guest house, caretaker's house, and stables housing his horses and fox hounds.

If anything bothered him, he thought his father-in-law could have given him a Cadillac or even a Mercedes, instead of the plebian Buick.

The house was grand and tastefully furnished in an understated but lush style that was a tribute to Anne's intelligence, taste, and character. The only serious mistake she ever made was marrying John. But hormones, emotions, alcohol, moonlight, and an instinct to punish her parents interfered with her otherwise excellent judgment.

John was casually sorting through the mail on the entry table when Anne came down the stairs, as always, coolly poised, neatly underdressed, immaculately groomed, and smiling.

"Care for a cocktail before dinner?"

"Cocktail sounds good. I'll have a dry martini on the rocks with a twist, but I can't stay for dinner. I'm just here to shower and change."

"Oh John! I planned a nice cool dinner on the terrace, and Dick and Delores Simpson are stopping by later for a drink and a swim."

"Sorry. I have to meet Nancy Schoen tonight and review the plans for the Charity Ball. We have to make a financial report and final recommendations."

"Oh, yes!," she replied archly. "You *have* to meet Nancy."

John was a lawyer. He loved argument the way an alcoholic loves the bottle. He was happy to engage her in the fashion he employed when baiting an opponent.

"Noblesse oblige, dear! No rest for the weary! Duty calls!"

"Who are you kidding? Nancy is a lady, and Harry is a special man. No one would believe she's your latest inamorata."

"Of course dear, if you say it's so, it must be so. Nancy is a lady and Harry is soooo special." He leered at her.

She placed a hand on his arm and made him look her in the face. "Darling, please stay home tonight."

He smiled slightly, patted her hand, and then gently lifted it and placed it on the table.

"No."

The look of anguish he wanted to elicit crept into Anne's eyes as he added the coup de grâce. "Don't wait up, I'll probably be late. Please have Lisa put the martini on the bedroom balcony. I'll have it after my shower." John ascended the stairs, leaving Anne to her imagination.

———•—•———

John Warden and Harry's wife, Nancy, had driven north along the winding Delaware River in Bucks County to the Black Walnut Hotel, a stately, colonial-era, Washington-slept-here fieldstone inn hidden away among the ancient oaks along the riverbank. It was difficult to imagine that this beautiful, tree-lined stream was the same turbid, freighter-loaded, reeking body of filth that oozed past the great port of Philadelphia only forty miles to the south.

Some tasty hors d'oeuvres on the screened terrace overlooking the river, some brittle conversation, a
little flattery, and a fair quantity of alcohol had Nancy
aglow. She looked lovely in the soft candlelight, which
emphasized her best features without revealing the
creases.

Nancy had begun to relax, the result of seeing
no one she knew, and quickly downing two top-shelf
Manhattans. She was relieved to see that the hotel terrace overlooking the Delaware River and the narrow
foot bridge spanning it to the New Jersey side were
deserted. She allowed herself to feel confident she
could manage to stay undiscovered. If she had been
recognized, Nancy had a ready explanation for being
seen with the family lawyer. She had rehearsed giving
it with a light and gay air: "Any sacrifice for charity!
John and I have the arduous task of selecting the restaurant for the hospital benefit."

She glanced up and discovered John's eyes study-
ing her. She flashed an embarrassed grin.

"This is asinine. I feel like a schoolgirl on a date,
instead of a broken down homemaker."

"I'm glad you feel like a schoolgirl, but I'm also
glad you look like an attractive, well-groomed, chicly-
dressed woman who is built like a terra cotta water
closet. Somehow, the idea of having cocktails with
freckles and pigtails does nothing for me."

Nancy smiled again, flattered to have the undi-
vided attention of an intelligent man. Harry was bet-
ter-looking than John, but she appreciated John's quick
wit, which ranged from sardonic to brittle, depending

on his mood. At least she was sipping cocktails in a lovely, romantic environment rather than standing in line at the supermarket, or chairing a mind-numbing country club tea.

But she was anxious nonetheless. "We really shouldn't have come here. There are many other people involved who could get hurt."

"You've been watching too many soap operas. I want you, and you want me to want you."

Nancy felt her face blazing.

"The only question is, Do you want me enough?" he continued. "I won't insult your intelligence by saying that I love you because I don't. I'm not sure that I'm even capable of love at all, but I do know that I would rather be here with you than with anyone else. You're unhappy. But the brass ring only goes by so many times. If you want something you have to grab it, and grabbing you is a delightful thought!"

Nancy surprised herself by putting her hand on his. "If I were ever to consider being grabbed, you would be the top selection."

He sandwiched her hand with his. "Nancy, I want you tonight." His voiced was husky with desire.

The sudden intensity startled her, but her own desire was rising. "I couldn't. Harry will be home for dinner. I have to be there."

"Call and tell Marcy you'll be late."

"I don't think I could."

"Of course you can. How many times has Harry been 'late?'" he said.

"Too damn many times. Okay. Harry and I are

having our problems, it's true. I'm sure you've noticed the awkwardness. But, believe it or not, I still enjoy being Mrs. Harry Schoen, and I intend to continue to be Mrs. Harry Schoen. I won't jeopardize my position."

"But you're trying to deny your own desires. We're mutually suited. You want to remain Mrs. Harry, I have to remain Mr. Anne. I have to, not for any noble reason such as the children, but for the cynically-practical reason that Anne's family is wealthy and social. The contacts it provides and the doors it opens are invaluable to my career, which is important to me.

"Furthermore, my father-in-law has decided that I'm to enter politics, which I happen to find almost as exciting as illicit sex. He's already mapped out my route: state senator, congressman, and then governor or senator. Divorce is not just out of the question, he wouldn't permit Anne to get one, no matter how much of a heel I might be."

Nancy was shocked by John's callous honesty and by her complete understanding and acceptance of his reasoning. After all, she was playing the same game with Harry.

"I luxuriate in the wealth that has dribbled down from Anne's family, and when I think about what's in the reservoir that may one day be mine to control and exploit—well, all my righteous indignation and upright moral fiber turns to dust.

"I'm a realist. I want the most with the least pain and simplest compromise. That means I remain married and continue to be your most discreet lover. I rest my case."

"You're an honest bastard."

"Rarely. But I'm here with you. That's as close to love as I'm capable. I want you tonight."

Nancy felt the telltale prickle of arousal. "In all honesty—rare for us women—my needs coincide with yours. I'll call and see if I can manage to be a little late for dinner. Mister, can you spare a dime?"

John sipped the last of his wine as he gazed with contentment at the river town of New Hope. He savored his conquest, perhaps even more than the second one he'd feel the moment he ejaculated into Nancy's body and would think, I've got you Harry, you bastard. I have cuckolded you. And the third, which would be when fellatio was completed.

He was a victorious general surveying the battle-field, oblivious to the bloodshed. He loved the law with equal passion because it satiated his need to feel superior by feeding upon the mistakes and inadequa-cies of others.

He purposefully targeted unlikely females for his games. They also had to meet a second qualification: their husbands had to be attractive men, often taller, younger, more athletic than he, and above all else, successful.

Nancy met all the requirements. Plus, she was friendly with his wife. For the next few months he would savor the relationship—the thrill of furtive trysts, the exultation of orgasm, the extra measure of pain in Anne's knowing eyes, the very special irony of sharing a drink with Harry and knowing he'd had the pleasure of his wife's body.

John was almost annoyed when Nancy's return broke his golden reverie. He smiled, but noticed she was frowning. "Problems?"

"No, no problems. In fact, we can have several extra hours. Harry's having dinner with his new boss. Could we get a room here tonight? It's so lovely, and I feel secure."

"Tried to, but it's booked up with New York tourists. I know a small motel across the river in Frenchtown. Believe me, no one goes to Frenchtown."

"Let's leave. It'll give us more time."

John nodded, but paused to slowly drain the dregs of his wine glass.

Nancy's passion was rooted in her anger at Harry. John was her weapon of choice. She might have been shocked to learn that she was also John's weapon of choice to punish Harry. The bed this evening would contain not two or four people, but three.

John had been considerate and skillful in bed—until she began to respond. Kee-rist! she thought when he put his tongue to work. It wouldn't have mattered if I were in bed with a St. Bernard.

She had had multiple orgasms and John had managed three, thanks to Harry. The last had been hard in coming, but the prolonged pumping had been great for her (oh, how good that little bit of soreness felt even now), and she accepted it as a challenge, which she successfully met by jabbing her nails into his buttocks and thrusting him in deeper while she gyrated her hips and moaned softly.

Nancy had only had two men in her life before

Harry, and only a few times. This had been her first dalliance since she married. She rated John a close second to Harry. He was better at oral sex, and seemed to take great delight in a slow, expert build-up, before she panted out her release.

Even with her great need today, she conceded that Harry was the better controlled, and the larger of the two. John had telegraphed his own desire to be gratified orally and, in spite of her normally strong reservations, she complied. He had thrust his cock in completely at the moment of release. She attributed his roughness to his great passion for her.

But the thought that crossed John's mind when he expelled his passion into Nancy's mouth was not of sexual joy, but gloating. I got you, Harry, you son-of-a-bitch. John smiled broadly as he pictured Harry kissing Nancy's mouth, and how he would feel the next time he met Harry.

He hated Harry—Harry the war hero, Harry the self-made man, Harry the self-assured. John had dodged the draft, married his money, and struggled with an inferiority complex that he hid behind an over-sized, abrasive ego.

Nancy and John rode home from the motel in silence. She was amazed at how she had been able to tap into the sensations of adolescence. She cuddled close to John, hugged his free arm, rested her head on his shoulder. "Oh John, it was a lovely evening." She stretched and felt the great sexual relaxation in her body, like a lioness who has just feasted after a difficult hunt.

Nancy sighed again, basking in the afterglow.

John couldn't wait to get rid of her.

He pulled alongside Nancy's car in the parking lot of the Black Walnut. "Sorry, Johnny," she said. "I have to run. But it was a wonderful evening, and you were wonderful for me."

He winced. Goddamned women always use the diminutive after you screw them. He said she was glorious and gave her a brushing kiss on the cheek.

"Call me tomorrow?" It was a request.

"Sure thing."

She smiled and the door slammed behind her.

He hoped Anne was still awake, so he could extract some additional pleasure from the evening. The thought made him a bit giddy, and he tried to compose some suitably witty lines.

Nancy let herself into the dusky house and flicked on the lights. She was still feeling the alcohol and took a hot shower, snacked out of the fridge, and brewed herself a strong cup of coffee. She sat on the screened-in patio in her robe, listening abstractly to the night sounds. Her head finally cleared, and the small vessel of guilt that the evening had launched now sank into the deep, vast sea of self interest, its fragile hull pierced by multiple rationalizations.

As if on cue, car lights cut an arc in the darkness, accompanied by the gravel crunch of the driveway. She followed Harry's progress through the house by the sounds of doors and footsteps. He would hang his suit coat in the entry way closet, deposit his attache case below, loosen his tie and remove his cuff links as he strolled toward the kitchen. She became apprehensive as he drew closer.

The refrigerator door closed—a snack, or ice for a highball, or both. She waited, preferring to receive him on the patio where the single citronella candle struggled to defeat the darkness. The door swung open as Harry, tie and collar loosened, cuffs rolled, entered with a scotch in hand. They eyed each other like rival tigers, trying to decide whether it was a good day to start a fight but both knowing their hearts weren't in it.

"Hi. Sorry I'm late. How was your day?"

"All right. Hungry? There's chicken."

"Thanks. I ate."

"Coffee?"

"No thanks. Where's Babs?"

"Party with the bridesmaids-to-be, at Stephanie's, I think. Rob drove her."

"Shouldn't you know where she is?"

"Is it pick-on-Nancy night? She's a big girl. Relax, 'Dad-Dee.' Your baby will be home soon." She tossed back the dregs of her coffee.

Harry rattled the ice in his glass. "I just love our intimate chats."

"Balls."

"Okay," Harry sighed. "Let's quit while we're behind. I'm bushed. G'night."

"Night."

Harry climbed the stairs and paused to linger in the doorway of Bab's room. It had its usual cluttered, but homey atmosphere. Nancy was right. He was having trouble comprehending her being married. His gaze drifted about the moonlit room, resting on a huge stuffed St. Bernard he had won for her a lifetime ago. He would never forget her uninhibited, wide-eyed joy as her hero placed the lop-eared toy in her arms.

On her dresser there was a photograph of the family at the shore on their cabin cruiser. There was a doll, ragged from being loved too well for too long and a dance program from her high school senior prom. A bottle of expensive perfume and a black bra hanging from a drawer attested to the passage of time and innocence lost. He sighed heavily.

How different the girls were. Ellen demanded love and reassurance. Babs drew it magnetically and effortlessly from others. She learned early that she was loveable and how to master the expressions and gestures that gave her an advantage. It had served her well as a child, but Harry worried that it could cause problems as a big girl, especially in matters where cute wouldn't cut it. In the end, he felt that he and Nancy had taught her enough self-regulation that she would be able to negotiate her life conscientiously.

———◦•◦———

Babs Schoen sat in the car waiting for her fiancé, Rob, to come back with the key. She felt so exposed sitting in front of a motel office, waiting for her lover. Rob returned and slipped into the seat, flashing his crooked, sexy smile. "Number eight, my lucky number. At the end of the row. Nice and private. Of course, all my numbers are lucky when I'm with you."

She squeezed his hand as he guided the car to the last unit. Babs leaned over and kissed him as he killed the engine and shut off the lights. The knob of the door to the next room rattled. The door swung open. Startled and feeling exposed, Babs opened her eyes.

A woman stepped out, framed by the light, followed by a man. Babs gasped. It looked like...it couldn't be, but it looked like her mother and . . . John Warden! The man switched off the room light and pulled the door shut.

Babs watched numbly over Rob's shoulder as the silhouettes merged on the motel porch for an instant, then stepped off the curb by a black Buick. The passenger door opened and this time she definitely saw her mother's neatly coiffed hair lit by the interior lights. She flashed into view a third time when John entered the driver's side. The engine cranked to life and the car pulled slowly away.

She was in stroboscopic shock.

"Babs? Babs? What is it honey?"

"I—I—don't feel so good all of a sudden. Could we just sit for a few minutes?"

"What is it? You were fine just a moment ago."

"Please!" The sudden note of fear in her voice startled him.

"Oh, honey," Rob said, puzzlement and worry mingling in his voice. "Did I do something wrong?"

Babs felt herself spinning. She thought she might actually lose her supper.

"No, no, no. It's nothing like that. Just.... Would

you mind if we just went home? I really feel kind of lousy."

"Well, I do mind. But you do look kind of pale. I'll take you straight home." He cranked the engine up and let out the emergency brake.

"No, let's go home the long way. I think a ride with the windows open may help."

———•••———

Alone again, Nancy was restless. She poured herself a rye and sat in the recreation room letting Johnny Carson distract her from her thoughts. She heard a car pull up and a key rattle in the front door.

"Babs? That you?" she called.

"Yes mother."

"I'm in here. How 'bout you and Rob join me for a nice little nightcap?"

"Rob went right home, and I'm going to bed." Nancy, the mother, heard something in Babs's voice she didn't like.

"Come here a minute, would you?" It was a command.

Babs entered the room tentatively. She was blushing and avoided her mother's eyes.

"What's the matter, honey?"

"Nothing."

"Oh, really? Come on!" She might be failing as a wife, but she could still be a warm, nurturing, intuitive mom who could cheer her little girl up by prying out the truth.

"You're home early, Rob doesn't come in to say goodnight, you're going right to bed, and nothing's wrong? You guys have a fight, or what?"

"Yes."

"Well, don't take it to heart, dear. Happens to every couple. Don't worry, you'll feel better in the morning."

"Yes mother. G'night."

Chapter Seven

A Pot-Hole in the Road

Harry sat in his office scowling at the detailed "BOB" plans for his department. Joe Graber had assured the management committee that supervisors would be consulted first. But Harry had been presented with a list of people to demote or fire. Either Graber had lied, or the blood letting was out of control as old scores were being settled. Harry couldn't decide which was worse.

He stared at the roster of victims. My God, he thought, if this plan is actually executed—the right word—it will be a terrible blow to Schopfer's morale. It was patently unfair. Middle managers and senior employees—who had generated the profits later squandered by inept "growth" plans—were going to pay for the sins of senior management.

The program was clearly aimed at culling older and more expensive employees. It was being conducted in a theatrical fashion that would shock the workforce and establish Graber as a tough boss, to be feared and obeyed. It was Darwinist—kill off the old, the sick, and the slow; the over fifty, high salaries, negative performance rating at any time in a career, or any negative comment by any supervisor. Prior merit or service was no defense. One "Oh shit!" carried as much weight as ten "Attaboys!"

The instructions for notifying the condemned and conducting the "separation interviews" were thorough and brutal. They had been drawn up by Graber's personal assistant, Alvin Boonberg, a moral piranha. He had poured all of his considerable intelligence, zeal, and malice into the documents. Harry underlined a few choice passages.

Personnel will be informed that they are being separated, because the company is upgrading its standards and they are not adequate. Upon separation, letters will be written to the personnel specifying their unsatisfactory performance.

It was a stupid thing to do, inflict pain without purpose. These people were not going to just vanish, Harry knew. They would reappear, probably at Schopfer's competitors. And they'd be in a really bad mood.

Harry groaned when, there on the list, was his former boss and benefactor: WINSTON, CHARLES S.

His secretary buzzed. "Mr. Schopfer on the line, sir."

"Harry, please stop up." Bobby barked.

Harry found Bobby sitting at his desk, drumming his fingers. "Now you understand what our luncheon conversation was about," Bobby said, waving a copy of the BOB plan. His mouth was pinched.

Harry nodded.

"Your opinion?"

Harry hedged. "Of course, I haven't had time to study it, but it does seem somewhat drastic. I trust there will be chances to discuss and modify some features."

"I'm afraid not Harry. Ernie and Joe are determined to push this right through as written, quickly." Bobby paused, searching Harry's face for a clue. "What do you really think it will do, Harry? In your personal opinion."

Harry looked evenly at Bobby, who was almost pleading for a response, praying for an escape hatch. His brain whirled. Bobby had said that Ernie and Joe were determined. This program looked like a disaster. His brain punched out an answer. Bobby—and only Bobby—could stop it. But, he asked himself, do you want to bet your ass on a resolute Bobby? Slice salami—take what you can get-mitigate and acquiesce. Maybe you can at least save Charley Winston, and some of the company morale.

"This program, or something close to it, has to be put through, Bobby. But it's drastic and it might be helpful to allow a few weeks for executives to study and comment on it."

Bobby's shoulders noticeably sagged as Harry spoke, and there was a small twinge about his eyes, as when a hypodermic is inserted. But he perked up when Harry added, "If you'd like, I could study the supporting draft memos and make comments for your consideration."

"Yes, yes," he nodded. "I'll get a complete copy for you and we'll analyze it together. Yes, yes! I'll ask Ernie for a draft."

"It might be better if you didn't say it's for me."

"Of course. The draft is for my personal use."

Ernst eyed the billow of smoke from his cigar and smiled with satisfaction. It had been a ritual lunch at the dining club, welcoming a new assistant vice president to the fold. Harry listened to the banalities and responded in kind, promising in essence to be loyal, brave, and true. Kind was not included. The waitress kept their cups full of coffee. Harry was relaxed, confident in his ability to handle such light conversation.

He let his attention wander, reflecting on the dining room as an outdated but pleasant relic. It had been the executive dining room for what had been regarded as an indestructible Philadelphia institution—the Curtis Publishing Company, publisher of some of the most popular magazines in the U.S., including its flagship, *The Saturday Evening Post.*

It was a monument to the inept marketing which had managed to destroy it, during a time when magazine industry sales were increasing but shifting from general interest periodicals such as the *Post* and their *Ladies Home Journal*, to specialized publications such as *TV Digest, Sports Illustrated, Motor Trend,* and *Teen.* A museum of its Norman Rockwell covers provided an idealized album of American mores, styles, and personalities. This "In Town Club" was a favorite haunt of Schopfer executives, on whom was lost the business lesson imbedded in its history.

Instead, they were seduced by its marble halls, carved oak furniture, crystal chandeliers, wooden phone booths the size of motel rooms, and excellent food served by its professional and obsequious staff. Women were, of course, excluded from its membership, and if they were brought to the club, were restricted to one small daintily decorated room.

Harry would have preferred a scotch or cognac to coffee, but Schopfer executives maintained the fiction that they avoided drinking at lunch—at least with each other.

"Harry." The tone in Ernst's voice startled Harry out of his reverie. "Harry, why did you ask Bobby to get you a copy of the 'Boost Our Business' Plan to study?"

Harry found himself uncharacteristically flustered. Ernst had set him up beautifully.

"I...I wanted it to...to consider it at Robert's request."

"One thing I have always liked about you was the way you kept your nose in your own business, and the fact that you were very careful not to trade on your friendship with my brother."

Harry was caught speechless.

"You just made Assistant VP, and a couple of days later you are ready to criticize plans made by Joe and me, and use your influence with Bobby to cause problems for no reason. Bobby confides in me about everything Harry, and he does what I tell him. Everyone at Schopfer does."

Harry opened his mouth to speak, but Ernst cut him off with a raised hand.

"I used to think you were bright. I might think so again, if you take the right attitude. You know a full VP slot will be opening up in a year or two, I was considering you for it."

Harry's mind was in disarray. Bobby's inability to resist Ernst's questions had done him in. The full weight of the importance of his career suddenly settled on him. The goal he had been so confident of attaining suddenly seemed to be slipping away. "Do something!" his brain commanded.

Harry surprised himself. "I appreciate your being direct. Now, I have a chance to explain myself." Ernst betrayed no emotion, other than a raised eyebrow.

"It's true that Robert sought me out several days ago. He was agitated. He would not say why, but he told me that something significant would happen at the next management meeting and he wanted me to pledge to give him my frank and personal opinion of it. I regretted that he put me on the spot, but I felt it would have been rude to turn down such a personal request, almost a plea, from someone I genuinely like."

"Oh?" said Ernst archly. "And why did you ask him for all the detailing memos and plans on a confidential basis?"

"Pull the trigger," came the brain's command.

"For three reasons: One, I wanted to give Robert the idea that he had my studied answer and that I was not casual about something that obviously was upsetting to him. Two, I wanted to have full knowledge of it so I could maneuver better for myself. And three, I wanted to find a loophole that would let me save Charley Winston's job.

He had to be completely candid with Ernst and he was employing the desperate "loaded gun" technique. This device is to be used in hopeless circumstances. You have a gun, but you are surrounded by armed thugs. You pick out their leader and hand your gun to him to hold for you while you bend down to tie your shoelace. The desperate theory being that he is less likely to shoot you with your own gun while you are completely defenseless.

Ernst sat back, took a pull on his stogie, and gave Harry an appraising look. "Well now, that sounds plausible. But tell me, what do you think you are going to tell Bobby?"

"Whatever you want me to tell him."

A shadow of a grin flickered across Ernst's lips. He leaned forward and pointed his cigar.

"Okay, Harry. I think we understand each other. You tell Bobby that the plan is hard but fair. You'll be allowed to offer Charley Winston a demotion to a district manager's job far away from Philadelphia—take it or leave it. For an old boozer like him, it's a break that'll keep him on his pension track.

"You're getting a new assistant who was personally selected by Bobby and Zelda, a fine young black man who just graduated from Wharton. For my part, I'm going to try to forget about this incident. It may take a year or two. Now, I'm going to linger here awhile."

Harry rose with a "Yes, sir," and left. He felt relieved and nauseated. He had stared into the abyss, where a wrong word can kill a career, but the price of redemption was so high. He had groveled and prostituted himself. Shit, it was Korea all over again. When the chips were down, you could count on bright, tough, knowledgeable Harry to turn ass and run. Twenty years later, and it still tormented his sleep and brought pain to his psyche when he reflected on his "heroism" in Korea. Now he was doing it all over again.

Ernst watched Harry's back as he left the dining room, leaned back, smiled, and released another cloud of cigar smoke. He wallowed in the afterglow of his power move. By habit, he removed the phone call slips from his pocket and glanced through them. Only the one from the managing editor of the *Philadelphia Times* puzzled him. Perhaps they wanted to do an article on a successful and civic-minded hometown company.

———————

"What's troubling you?" Marie stroked Harry's hair.

"Can't hide anything from you," he muttered from the adjoining pillow.

"You've been too smiley and animated tonight—at least right up to the time we got into bed. You're no more interested in making love to me than you are in running the Boston Marathon."

"Sorry. It's not you."

After swearing her to secrecy, he told her about the BOB plan, and what it meant for Charley Winston.

"How terrible for all those people like Charley. "Uh... What about my job?"

"You're okay. It's mostly aimed at older, more expensive professionals."

"Don't they realize this'll hurt morale?"

"Yes."

Harry paused. "Robert also mentioned a health problem at Bridesburg. You know anything about that?"

Marie nodded. "No one's supposed to, but the bosses always treat us clerks and secretaries like furniture. They forget that we're actually paying attention when we're typing memos, copying documents, and filing. The same for their chauffeurs, while they're chatting in the back seat. We peons have a great word-of-mouth communication system."

"Tell me about it."

"Well, I don't really know anything definite, but it sounds like some people at a production building—R5—were maybe getting sick and even dying of lung cancer, and they think it might have something to with some hot gases that made them cough. It's all supposed to be hush-hush."

That squared with what Bobby had alluded to—a respiratory issue, lung cancer. "Sounds serious."

"Well, lover, I always worry about chemicals and what they might do to me."

Harry felt compelled to defend his profession and his career. "I've always been proud to be a chemist, and to work for Schopfer. All things that bring benefits to people also carry risk. Look at aspirin. It's a deadly poison with no known antidote. It causes ulcers and gastro-intestinal bleeding. It's got a nasty-sounding chemical name—acetyl salicylic acid. But it's been a boon to mankind.

"In spite of industrial pollution, life spans keep increasing and our oldsters seem surprisingly spry relative to those of our childhood memories, thanks to research on those chemicals we call medicines. Remember, the mortality rate will always be a hundred percent. My bottom line is that religion helps people die better, and science helps them live better."

Harry's intensity surprised Marie, and charmed her. She kissed and hugged him. "Well, I'm sure that if there's a real problem at Bridesburg, the company will deal fairly with it."

Chapter Eight

Two Close Shaves

Charley Winston blinked and his hands balled into fists as Harry explained that, after thirty-seven years of loyal service with Schopfer, instead of being promoted, he was to be demoted to district manager of a minor office in Oregon. Harry's stomach churned as he added, "The only option is to resign. I'm really sorry. It's out of my hands."

"Some God-damn choice, Harry," Charley growled. "I'm fifty-eight years old. What kind of a job can I get? You're too young to have investigated it, but you know that wonderful pension plan we always hear about? Well, like most of them, it's got loopholes. All those nice secure income numbers you hear about are for age sixty-five and the pension vesting funds go up geometrically as you approach sixty-five. So if you retire early—say about seven years early—you get peanuts.

"Why the hell do you think they went gunning for people over fifty in this stinking BOB program?"

Harry felt like he was shrinking. "I feel shitty about this, but it's the best I could do. The alternative was even worse. This way I could at least save your pension, and I'll give your reassignment a good cover memo."

Charley scowled, baring his teeth like a cornered animal. "Yeah, those long memos that tell you that the fellow had his balls chopped off. The demotion means reduced salary and of course the final pension is based on salary for the last five years of employment."

"I'm sorry." Harry wondered if one day people would say of him what he had sometimes said of others, that he had climbed the corporate ladder by stepping on the hands of others.

Charley sagged, suddenly looking older, much older. "I know, Harry. It's just hard to be cheerful when you've just been kicked in the balls, even by a friend."

Charley's eyes shone with emotion. Harry felt his own throat tightening. In the male world of their generations, Harry did the most he could; he leaned across his desk and put his hand on Charley's forearm.

The touch had a galvanic effect on the older man. He quickly squared his shoulders, rose to his full height, and said in a crisp, resonant voice, "Well that's it. Many thanks. Take care of yourself, Harry." Then he turned toward the door.

"We'll be seeing each other, Charley."

"Sure we will."

Harry needed a drink, so he left the office early.

———·•·———

"Harry, please hurry. We're due at the club by seven o'clock and I can't be late." Nancy's voice was edgier than usual. She was chairwoman of the charity dinner dance at the New Hope Country Club and she would be judged on every detail. Harry knew from years of experience that she would be uptight until the moment they arrived. She would then miraculously become the relaxed, charming, gracious, confident director of the evening. He also knew that when it was over she would collapse into a heap of exhausted insecurity and cross-examine him for a critical review, never quite believing his assurances of her excellent performance.

He lathered his beard and began shaving. As he looked at himself in the mirror, he saw again the awful injured, helpless look in Charley Winston's eyes. He felt a fresh flush of shame as he dabbed at a nick on his chin. The sight of droplets of blood on the billowy-white shaving cream in the sink unleashed a wave of goosebumps.

———◦·•·◦———

On a crisp, clear night in the Korean hills, the temperature had bottomed at thirty degrees below zero. The old saw, that once it goes below zero it doesn't matter, is a crock. The body groans with each degree lost. At least the air was still. Otherwise the medics would have been swamped with cases of frostbite.

The light from the quarter moon and luminous stars was reflected by the snow, just enough to enable the troops to move about without stepping in holes, tripping, or walking into trees.

Private Phillips, an eighteen-year-old from the Tennessee hills, manned a listening post on the edge of the battery area and listened for any sign of the enemy. The 105-millimeter howitzer battalions were about two miles behind the front line.

A Republic of Korea (ROK) infantry battalion protected their front. But, as acting battery commander, Lt. Harry Schoen was taking no chances. He made sure the perimeter was well maintained, with interlocking fields of fire, patrols, sentries, listening posts, ready reserves sleeping in the headquarters area, periodic phone reports from every post, inspections by the sergeant and officer of the guard, flares and grenades on trip wires, and C-ration cans with pebbles inside hung from barbed wire to alert the sentries if the wires were jostled.

Phillips sat in his hole, with the A-6 30-caliber light machine gun, violently shivering. "Stay put and keep quiet," the sergeant had ordered. But the nerves on the skin were screaming, "Too cold!" and the brain was screaming at the body, "Exercise to warm up!" Phillips fought to keep himself still, but he lacked the Arctic gear that the Army, in its wisdom, determined was not necessary in this temperate zone.

The bitter cold had come as suddenly as the Chinese, just when it appeared they had the war wrapped up. Phillips shifted the scarf covering his nose and mouth periodically to break off the ice formed by his breath.

Lt. Col. Lowe's jeep jolted along the snowy tracks, up, down, and side to side. He hung on to the hand grips and tried to compose the few words he would leave behind with Charlie Battery. Lowe regretted that the Chinks came from this end of the battalion, where he had a lightly experienced R.O.T.C. 2nd Lt. in command—Harry Schoen.

The battery commander had been sent back with pneumonia two days before. On the other end he had Able Battery, led by an up-from-the-ranks World War II artillery veteran, Capt. Smiley. Lt. Schoen had done a decent job for a few months as exec, and Gulley was satisfied with his performance running the fire direction center for the battery. Whether Lt. Col. Lowe liked it or not, Lt. Schoen was going to have to lead the battalion defense against the advancing Chinese.

The driver braked the jeep to a skidding stop outside the squad tent housing the Fire Direction Center. Lowe stepped out on the ice, trying to stamp some feeling back into his toes. Harry's head poked out through the flap, but Lowe waved him back in. The dripping gasoline heater made the interior bearably warm, but the air was rank with exhaust fumes and human stench.

Lowe removed his trigger-finger mittens and motioned Harry past the horizontal and vertical firing chart manned by a bleary-eyed G.I. An equally bleary-eyed soldier sat at a small table with a slide rule, computing the howitzer fire. The guns were spread in their revetments over a hundred yards in the classic "Lazy W" pattern. They had been shooting up a storm for hours in support of the hard-pressed Korean infantry in front. For the moment, the guns were silent.

Lowe pulled out the situation map he'd brought with him. "Bad news, Lieutenant. The ROK regiment on your right flank broke and the Chinks are coming down our little valley. There's only this one trail out, between you and Baker.

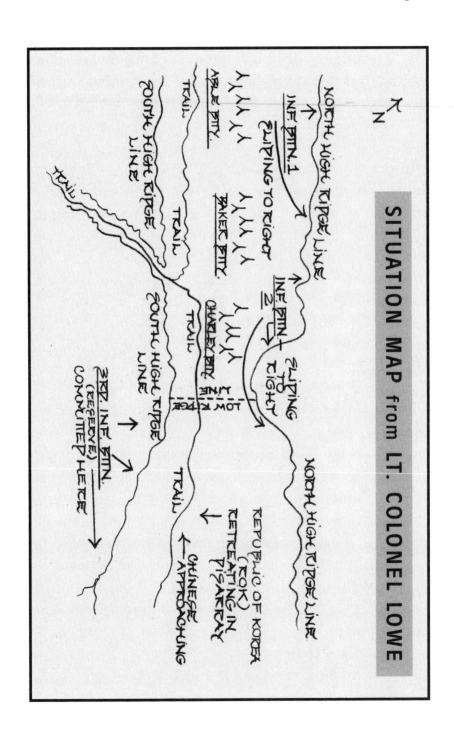

SITUATION MAP from LT. COLONEL LOWE

"The reserve infantry battalion is moving up these heights on the southern ridge to hold for awhile. The 1st and 2nd Battalions have spread themselves thin to stretch over past the rise to your right.

"Between them and the reserve battalion, you shouldn't have to worry about your flanks. After the artillery—including you—is out of here, the First and Second Infantry will retreat across the valley to take up positions on the southern ridge line. You're going to be the cork in the bottle. You've got to hold them for a few hours while we get Able, Baker, and Service out on that trail. After that, you're to withdraw under cover of barrages as soon as they're set up in new positions.

"You've got to hold this position to save the asses of our battalion and the two infantry battalions on the north ridge."

Harry pored over the map, tracing the ridge line with his finger. The heater sputtered and hissed in the silence.

"I see sir. We'll do our damnedest. I sure could use some more firepower. How about a couple of twin 40mm mounts, and a couple of quad-50 machine gun mounts from that triple A outfit back here." Harry stabbed at a location on the map.

"If it can be done, I'll get them for you Schoen."

"Any tanks with the Chinks?"

"Not yet, but they may be here before they attack. Let's hope not."

"Yes sir, let's hope not."

"We'll flag you out as fast as we can. Good luck, lieutenant."

Lowe stepped out of the tent and shivered. Poor

bastards, he thought, recalling memories of himself as a young inexperienced lieutenant, a member of the Ninth Infantry Division, staring down a phalanx of Rommel's tanks in the Kassarine Pass. He would never forget the slaughter visited on the men in his artillery unit.

As the jeep sped away in the darkness, Harry cranked the field phone, shouting for all section chiefs and other non-coms to come to the fire direction tent, on the double.

As they gathered in a circle, he briefed them with Lowe's map. Not a squawk from the men, but Harry noticed many eyes lowered. His sturdy first sergeant broke the awkward silence. "Yes sir! How do you want us deployed?"

Harry laid out a series of orders. "Section chiefs shift trails ninety degrees to the right. We're going to hold them at that rise about two thousand yards down from our right flank. Make sure you can all bore sight where the trail comes through the rise. Any armor will have to use it.

"Fire direction, lay out a walking barrage on the reverse slope, to hold down the number of chinks who get to our side.

"Lay out lots of variable time fuses, white phosphorous, have some armor piercing ready, and some canister if they get real close."

The briefing lasted fifteen minutes. Harry left nothing to chance, describing every detail and every response to every eventuality. As the men bustled about preparing for the battle, Harry cranked up division artillery headquarters to put in his firing request.

"Hello, Schoen," the brigadier general answered. "Got yourself a hot spot, I hear."

"Yes sir, but I want to request that all available units lay out this position from here to the rise and monitor frequency Zeta for the command, 'Joe DiMaggio,' when I want them to shell my position."

"Let's hope that won't be necessary, lieutenant."

"I certainly hope not sir, but it might buy some time to get more troops out by the trail."

"Okay son, just about everything we got is moving now, but I'll make a general order for all units to plot you out first thing when they set up and monitor Zeta. Best of luck."

———••——

Harry awoke to find his driver shaking him. "Lt. Schoen—it's startin' suh." Harry was startled to find that he had fallen asleep on a metal chair sitting in the Fire Direction Center Tent.

Just before dozing off, Harry remembered how, as a youth, he had been stirred by the tale of the noble Roland fighting and dying in a rear guard action at a bridge to allow Charlemagne's army to escape the Saracens. Harry didn't feel noble right now. His stomach ached.

Private Phillips, the driver, quickly filled Harry in: "Forward listening posts report voices all around them. Right point just reported noise on the wire, likely a Chink patrol."

Harry looked up to the fire direction operators,

who were staring at him with wide eyes. "Start the walking barrage."

Within seconds, six howitzers roared as one, spewing five foot flames into the black sky.

"Brown, crank up regimental HQ" Harry's voice had assumed a quiet, even tone.

"Radio, call HQ battery, alert Able and Baker's batteries, fill them in, tell them to cover their own asses and be ready to light us up with star shells and close in fire as soon as they reach their new positions."

"Regimental HQ on the phone sir. It's Major Lueke."

"Hello sir." A distant blast of a hand grenade set off by a careless foot snagging a trip wire interrupted. "Sir, it's starting. I'm shooting the reverse slope, but they'll be over soon, sure could use some infantry with mortars."

"Jesus, Lieutenant, I've only got one platoon in reserve for the whole regiment and they're mostly cooks and clerks. I can't spare them unless you're going under. Do your best, and keep me posted. Out." The phone went dead.

Bugle calls rang throughout the valley. It was the Chinese version of psychological warfare, to frighten their opponents. The sound usually was followed by a "human sea" attack by overwhelming numbers.

The whoosh of incoming mortar rounds started as Harry slid across the snow and into a hole. His young hillbilly driver, Phillips, had already slapped a belt of rounds into the 30-caliber machine gun and pulled the bolt. "Yawl want to feed or shoot, suh?"

"You shoot, Phillips. Just pretend it's a Tennessee

turkey shoot."

"Yes suh, but they never did shoot back."

"Scared, Phillips?"

"Yes suh, I already pissed my pants."

Harry laughed, "You won't be the only one."

Rifles now crackled all around them. The muzzles spit brilliant flames. The burst of Russian AK-47s and the mortar blasts became heavier, closer. Unfortunately, the Chinese were very good with mortars.

Star shells began to light the front of Charley's position as the flares drifted down on their parachutes. The din grew to a ferocious level and the ground shook repeatedly as Harry peered around the semi-circle of the battery's defensive front. He gasped as he saw what appeared to be a sea of Chinese surrounding three sides of their position and coming on despite the fire. Friendly artillery rounds started falling within fifty yards of the wire, tearing craters, raining clods of dirt, and throwing bodies into the air.

Phillips continued firing and the hot steel of the gun emitted an oily aroma. Harry fed the belt mechanically as he looked around the scene. Fire came in from all directions. A mortar round hit close behind one of the howitzers and the crew went down.

He saw the sergeant dash for the cannon, pulling three men out of foxholes to join him on the way. He went down with blood spurting from his chest, but the other three made the relative safety of the gun's shield and started cranking out rounds point blank into the oncoming Chinese. Cannon rounds ricocheted off the frozen ground with a sound like a racing locomotive.

Some Chinese reached the final line of barbed

wire to the right, where they drew a brief concentration of fire and withered away. Harry left Phillips and dashed behind what was left of the Fire Direction Control tent.

"Okay, men, take the 30-caliber machine gun and the rocket launcher and fill that gap over there." One man remained still as the others set off, and Harry slid into the hole to send him off, only to be greeted by the unwavering stare of the boy's unseeing eyes. A small hole in his helmet had leaked a trail of blood on the side of his head.

Harry began to shake. He turned away abruptly and shook his head like a fighter trying to clear his thoughts. Nothing more to do now, he thought. No more reserves, no more orders. Everyone was fighting to save his own ass and there was nowhere to go.

The Chinese were all over the wire now, so close that hand grenades were beginning to bounce in. The radio squawked in the shredded remains of the tent: "Crucible to Wayside Charlie, this is Paddock Two. Give a status report."

Harry slithered under the edge of the collapsed tent and reached up and grabbed the radio mike. "Wayside Paddock! This is Charlie Two. That ain't Harry James blowing those bugles you hear. Get off the air, you cocksucker. We're going under."

Harry barked out the order that would unleash the last-ditch defense—friendly fire raining down on his position. "All units. All units. This is Charlie Two, Joe DiMaggio." Came the response, "Get your heads down. We'll be on you."

Harry crouched low, slunk along, and made it

back to the foxhole. Phillips was still on the machine gun, but the last belt was already feeding through.

"Be down to our carbines soon," he yelled at Harry as a grenade exploded just to their front. The force of the blast blew Harry against the back edge of the hole and he felt a searing sensation in his left leg. Phillips lay next to him bleeding from several spots.

Harry struggled forward and fired a burst from his carbine at two Chinese soldiers just ten yards away. They fell back.

"Phillips, come on!" He shook him. "C'mon kid! We got to get out of here and move back by the guns." Phillips managed to prop himself up.

"Give me my carbine," he demanded.

Harry handed it to him. "Come on kid, let's go."

"Ah cain't. Ma legs won't move."

Harry grasped the boy under the arms and tried to draw him out of the hole, but with his own left leg useless and Phillips' dead weight, he couldn't budge him. Harry began to whimper in frustration. "Come on kid, try."

"Ah cain't."

Harry took an extra carbine banana clip from his belt, thrust it into the boy's hands, and slithered out the rear, trying not to look into his terrified eyes. "Hang on kid! I'll get help."

As Harry scuffled away, he heard a voice from the foxhole: "Mama, mama."

The 105 rounds Harry had called for began pounding their sister battery's position. Harry knew the supporting theory for the action—the friendly fire should kill more foe than friend. But it was a bitch to reflect upon the logic while he was sitting where the rounds were falling. The volume of artillery increased in number and shell size. Harry guessed that the eighteen guns of the 155mm battalion had joined in. Thank you, General Theimer.

Harry managed to retreat about twenty-five yards into a shallow depression. He lay there shaking violently, while the roar of the battle continued on. He wanted to find somebody, anybody, to go back for Phillips. He called out "Medic!" several times, but his voice was drowned out by the battle roar. He was paralyzed by pain, shock, cold, loss of blood.

Through the din a new sound emerged—tracked armored vehicles were coming. The roar of the two quad 50-caliber machine gun mounts assured Harry that they belonged to the right side. Four thousand rounds per minute now hosed down the battle site, tipping the scales. They were soon joined by two twin 40mm mounts, each pouring out two hundred and forty air exploding rounds a minute, scattering shrapnel like red hot snow flakes.

The Chinese began to move away, slowly at first, then turned and fled in panic. The star shells lighted them well as the three remaining functional guns in the battery switched back from canister to variable time fuses and chewed up the Chinese who tried to scurry over to the relative security of the reverse slope. The quad 50s and the twin 40mms exacted a fearsome toll on the retreating soldiers.

"Phillips! Phillips!" Harry began to crawl the reverse route to the foxhole. As he approached, he saw several more dead Chinese than the two he had wasted.

"Phillips! Phillips!" But the hole did not respond. He looked down, and the tears started to trickle down his face, turning muddy as they mingled with the grime and fell as small blots on the incredibly white, sterile snow.

The boy lay on his side, but the bayonet wound was apparent; it had entered low, about the navel, and ripped obliquely upward for about eight inches. Intestines oozed out of the gap and one frozen hand grasped them in an attempt to hold them inside where they belonged. He forced himself down in the hole and placed his ear against the chest of the lad, but heard no sound or motion. "Medic! Medic!" he screamed.

He was still screaming when they got to him several minutes later, and Sergeant Gibson, with a soothing soft voice, tried to console him. "Don't worry Sir. We'll take good care of him."

He pried Harry's fingers and arms from the corpse's shoulders. He lifted Harry and carried him up out of the hole toward the spot where the medics were feverishly shooting morphine, bandaging, applying tourniquets, or slowly pulling ponchos over faces.

Harry lay looking at the beautiful star-lit sky floating peacefully above. Gibson's voice drifted through as he talked on the pack radio. "Jesus Christ, the old man and Phillips must have wasted about twenty Chinks right on the edge. Looks like they ran out of 30 ammo and did it with carbines and grenades. They saved our asses!"

Harry closed his eyes, but the tears continued to escape from the corners.

———•———

Harry lay in the hospital bed in the white sheets, smelling of antiseptic. He scowled and watched the smoke drift away from his cigarette. He had just completed the odious duty of writing thirty-five letters to wives and parents in a feeble attempt to console them on the loss of the husbands and sons under his command. His last letter was for Phillips's parents. He told them how well-liked he had been, how courageous, and how his last words had been for his mother. Harry omitted that he felt that he should have died with him.

"Lt. Colonel Lowe to see you," a nurse announced.

"How are you feeling, Schoen?"

"Leg's a little stiff, but everything is in working order."

"Well, it's a million dollar wound, anyway. It's going to get you back to the States and out of the Army, if you want out."

"I want out, sir. No disrespect intended, but it is not what I do best."

"You did pretty well, Harry, if I may call you that. In fact I have a present for you." He handed over a small box with single silver bars in it, and gave a small salute as he said, "May I be the first to call you 1st Lt. Schoen. Major Lueke was mad at you for calling him a cocksucker, but under the circumstances, it sounded reasonable to me. Rather than a court-martial, I'm afraid I've recommended you for a silver star to go with the purple heart."

"But sir, it was a unit action, not—."

"I've talked with Sergeant Gibson and he said that it was your action on the point that held your perimeter together long enough, when combined with calling down your own artillery."

Harry appeared stunned, and then anger flushed his face. "Sir, I had thirty-five men killed and only twelve wounded. Do you know why that ratio was so high? Because most of the wounded were bayoneted to death when we were overrun, and we wouldn't have been, not if I had gotten help when I first asked for it."

His voice now dropped to a hoarse whisper. "Bring Major Lueke around. I'll call him a cocksucker to his face."

With a look of sadness, Lowe rose slowly. "Lt. Schoen, you are a brave man, and you have done an excellent job for your country and your men. For these things, I honor and thank you. However, as a soldier you are an amateur. You lost thirty-five men, you poor son-of-a-bitch! How many do you think Major Lueke sends to their deaths! Your action likely saved several hundred lives for the rest of our battalion and for the infantry.

"This is your first and last war, this is my second and probably not my last. You college boy civilians sit on your asses and get wealthy while the press makes fun of us professionals until the bell rings and we get our asses shot off saving yours.

"So maybe Major Lueke made a mistake, in hind-sight, but that's too fucking bad. How many decisions involving lives do you think he makes a week? Don't you think he knows when he's wrong? Don't you think he bleeds inside when the casualties come in?"

Harry blushed with shame. "I'm...I'm sorry sir. I... I just...."

"That's all right. I didn't mean to make a speech. It's just that fellows like you don't really understand the system and know what's necessary. You think all those little chicken-shit orders and regulations are just that. Without discipline you could never get sane men to stand up and follow you up a hill under fire. You can't stop and take a vote. They just have to go. Obedience has to become a habit.

"I'll let you in on an open secret, Lieutenant: after a battle, all the survivors feel guilty, because they are alive and their friends are dead. And they remember that their first thought likely was, 'I'm glad it was them instead of me.'"

Lowe extended his hand, saying, "Best wishes, Lieutenant, and you are still going to get that silver star."

"Thanks for the lesson, sir. I mean that, sir. But I have a request to make."

"Yes?"

"Could the medal go to Private Phillips, sir?"

I have already recommended him for a posthumous award of a Bronze Star. It was a noble offer, but I'm afraid you'll have to accept one also."

"Yes sir."

Lowe wheeled and vanished. Harry lit another cigarette, laid his head back on the pillow, and stared, unseeing, at the ceiling. Phillips would be with him all the days of his life. He would be sure to appear at

Harry's death bed, smiling his boyish, friendly, open grin and trying to hold his bloody guts from falling out.

———•◦✦◦•———

"Harry! Harreeee! What are you doing, day-dreaming in front of the mirror when we're in such a hurry!"

"All right Nancy, I'll be right with you," Harry answered flatly.

"Damn," thought Nancy, "there he goes, off in another blue funk just when I need him."

●

Chapter Nine

Dance Cards and Bad Hands

Harry stood at the bar nursing a drink and surveying the large, circular ballroom of the New
Hope Country Club. A bandstand intruded at
the far side with six tuxedoed musicians grinding out
desultory renditions of "Tea For Two," "Deep Purple,"
and occasionally a gourd-shake attempt at a Latinesque
Lombardo-ized version of an Xavier Cugat number.

He had watched with detached interest as Nancy
stood with John Warden and the rest of the committee at the reception hall entrance, smiling broadly and
greeting the last stragglers with exaggerated gestures
and facial expressions. Unable to hear what was being
said, the scene bore a silent movie quality.

The bar was midway between the all-penquin
band and the group of penguins and butterflies at the
reception line. Directly across the room, French doors
led to a large elevated patio with balustrades, benches,
and Grecian urns surrounded by well-tended rose
bushes in full bloom. Tables were scattered throughout
the room, on lush blue carpeting. A small, highly polished parquet dance floor surrounded the bandstand.

The crowd was predictably older, sporting the

gray hair and tanned skin of the leisure class—dressed in designer gowns, *After Six* tuxedos, and dinner jackets with black or maroon cumberbunds.

As the evening evolved, the revelers dropped their reserved demeanors and became rather boisterous. Harry noted that alcohol always seems to impair hearing, making it necessary to converse loudly. The dancers became slightly salacious and some theatrical steps and dips appeared as the matrons became maidens and remembered how Ginger had done it, while the men lightly aped Fred.

Just as Nancy had observed, Harry had arrived in a low mood, a combination of the nick on his chin, which he touched occasionally, and the appearance of the ghosts of his failings in war and business, which seemed to garner him unmerited awards.

He had been betrayed by his old friend alcohol. He had been consuming steadily, but with little effect. He found no middle ground of ease this night. He could have remained largely and painfully sober, or gone about the business of getting bombed. In this mood, he would have chosen the latter in private, but stuck with the former in this public display. His Army-developed tolerance of the drunk by the sober had faded with the passing years. He now suffered the discomfiture of the clear-headed civilian surrounded by the fairly intoxicated. Civilians must always get drunk together at the same rate, or they will offend each other.

The events of the evening had not helped. Harry noticed Charley Winston drinking heavily, and became concerned that Charley was headed back into the problem that he had early in his career, the problem which likely provided Harry with the opportunity to surpass him on the steps to success.

Harry approached Charley's wife Agnes, who was giving tight little brave smiles by his side, and drew her away.

"Oh Harry, I'm scared. Charley hasn't drank like this in years, and he's been so down since the demotion." She paused, then quickly added, "but I want to thank you for saving his job."

He waved off her gratitude, although he knew it was genuine. As a corporate-wise wife, she could look at the names of those who had been axed and realize that Charley would have been among them, if not for Harry.

"I've been trying to make it an exciting adventure, talking up the idea of getting out from under a big suburban house, buying a condominium and taking up a new lifestyle. But I know that he feels rejected and cast off, and underneath, perhaps a failure."

"Would you like me to try to get him to leave?"

"Oh yes, Harry! Could you?"

Charley was holding court, surrounded by a group of men and a few women enjoying his masterful retelling of classic stories. His voice inflections, accents, and timing were superb. Charley was an entertainer. Harry waited to approach until Charley's Irish brogue tale about two gay men named Patrick Fitzhugh and Hugh Fitzpatrick ended in gales of laughter.

"Excuse me, Charley. May I speak with you for a moment?"

"Scuse me folks, duty and boss call."

They walked a few steps away from the crowd. "I've

been having trouble seeing you at work, Charley."

"Well I'm busy wrapping things up and getting ready to move."

"Well, how about lunch on Monday?"

"I'm not sure if I'm open Harry. I'll call you." He started to move back toward his waiting audience.

Harry placed an arm on Charley's shoulder to restrain him. "Charley, how about taking Agnes home now."

Charley stopped and looked Harry in the eye. "What you are really saying is stop drinking now."

"Perhaps."

"Is that a work order or a social request?"

"A request."

"Then stuff it. I don't need to be sober to be a D.M. in Oregon. That job I could handle from a phone in a bar. Besides, you know good old Charley—when things go awry, he goes a rye." He winked and walked away.

Agnes took Charley's arm and stole a glance at Harry who discreetly shook his head.

———•◦•———

Harry had been approached earlier in the evening by Robbie's father, who'd asked if he and his wife could stop by the house to discuss something important. They declined to name the topic and Harry knew better than to pry. They agreed they would meet after the dance.

As the evening wound down, Nancy was still

going strong, visiting tables, congratulating people for their efforts, thanking others for their donations, propping up an ego here, flattering a body there, politicking for her next campaign for office. Harry made the mandatory visits with her, posed for pictures for the local newspapers, and danced several times. But largely he had floated around the edges giving naughty insignificant responses to the unsubtle advances of some of his wife's acquaintances.

He spent as much time as possible on the patio to escape the crowd. Harry noted that Nancy, once again, was dancing closely with John Warden. It was natural for the co-chairpersons who had done all the work to celebrate their success together. Nancy looked radiant and happy. Even John, normally somewhat stiff and pompous, had been expansive this evening, greeting Harry with gusto and pushing him together with Nancy when John and Anne joined them for the benefit of the photographers. John even suggested a congratulatory kiss pose.

Nancy smiled and waved to a couple on the club steps as Harry tipped the valet and slipped behind the wheel. Nancy slumped down in the seat as soon as the Cadillac cleared the driveway and entered the road. The nervous energy had drained her of all her reserve. She immediately began expressing the customary doubts and self-recriminations. "The damn shrimp were rubbery and that new bartender acted like he was doing people a favor to serve them, the bastard."

"The shrimp were fine and I heard nothing but praise for the affair, so relax."

"Relax? Yes, I think I will. I'm bushed, but I'll

have to remember to call all the committee members tomorrow and thank them personally, as well as Mrs. Webster to apologize."

"Why her?"

"The old biddy didn't like her table and told me about it. Too close to the kitchen door. Fortunately the Williamses, that new couple who are trying to establish themselves, were only too happy to switch."

"Maybe, just maybe, they were trying to be genuinely helpful."

"You are naive Harry. Mrs. Williams will be helpful to me for the next year or so, but she's ambitious. I'll have to keep an eye on her. But for now I'm going home, shower, pop a pill, take the phone off the hook, and sleep until noon."

"You deserve it Nancy. You did a beautiful job on the dance. But I'm afraid you'll have to wait a few minutes. Art and Helen are going to stop by."

"What for?"

"I don't know but Art said they had to see us and he wouldn't elaborate."

Babs and Rob had taken a cabin at a small motel up the river. Rob had suggested the place in Frenchtown, but Babs had flatly turned it down. Babs chuckled as she wiggled out of her Lord & Taylor evening dress and let it collapse into a soft mound on the carpet. A neon glow leaked around the cheap drapes and reflected in her wide eyes. Rob's hands slid appreciatively down her smooth skin and rested on her hips, his arms extended at full length so that he could view her firm, young body. "Oh Rob, I've got two hours with you. How lovely."

Rob grinned and pulled her to him. "Love you," he whispered in a soft monotone. His brow creased, "Are you sure that your mom and dad won't miss you?"

"Oh, don't worry. As chairlady, mom will have to stay until the bitter end of the dance, and daddy trusts his little girl."

"You don't feel like a little girl."

"You don't feel like a little boy."

After their lovemaking, they lay in bed. Rob drew on a cigarette, watching the end glow in the dark. He felt good.

"Rob-ee?"

"Yes."

"How is the job going? Are you getting along with your dad?"

"Oh, he's okay. The work isn't too bad. It's just that he's a bird on the idea of service. He turns himself inside out to help a client—takes all kinds of weirdo phone calls at all hours and hustles out to console some character who's had a kitchen fire or accident. He even calls on widows after the funerals—sends a sympathy card first—and provides a typed statement of their benefits." He shook his head. "He is something else," he said with a mixture of amazement and puzzlement, and a tinge of admiration.

"Can you imagine he expects the same of me?"

Rob went on in a mock-stentorian voice, "'Son, the

only thing that distinguishes an insurance agent from a coin operated machine or a mail-in coupon is service. People in trouble don't want to leave phone messages. They need to speak promptly with a person. You have a chance to be genuinely helpful to them, just like their doctor, lawyer, or minister. They are in trouble and upset and you can help.'

"I just can't pretend to be all shook up because some old biddy has a dented fender and wants me to run out to see her. But that's the part that gets me. I don't think he has to pretend. He really is concerned!"

Babs loved listening to Rob talk. "Are you sure you really want to stay in the business? Wouldn't you rather go back to Bucknell and finish up your degree?"

"Hey honey, I thought we had this all settled."

"Yes, but I feel guilty. You dropping out of college and coming here to marry me rather than doing what you wanted."

"Don't feel that way, honey. I want to marry you."

"But we could be married and you could still go back to school. I could get a job and we could have a little apartment off-campus until you get your degree. I know our fathers would help us."

"Forget it honey. I'm never going back to Bucknell. I'm staying here with you."

"But it wouldn't be for too long. You're only a couple of months short of finishing your junior year. I wish you had waited those two months."

Rob pulled his arm from around Babs' shoulder and sprang off the bed. "I said forget it, and I mean that! I never want to hear about it again, understand?"

he growled.

"No, I don't understand, but I won't mention it again if that's the way you want it."

"That's the way I want it."

Babs turned her head toward the wall as a tear tracked its way down her cheek. Rob softened instantly and went to her side. "I'm sorry honey. It's just that I spent a lot of time considering all this, and it is resolved. Okay?"

"Okay."

"Now give me a kiss. I had better get you home. It's about break-up time for the country club set."

Young love, with only two participants in the bed, seems sweet and uncomplicated.

Rob's parents, Art and Helen Hawthorne, arrived at the Schoen home minutes behind Harry and Nancy. They were both fidgety and refused drinks, choosing to sit side by side on the couch, hands clasped in their laps. Harry leaned against the mantle while Nancy did her best to smile from her perch in an easy chair.

Art began, "This is difficult for me, but I feel responsible for informing you, and the sooner the better."

Harry and Nancy said nothing, but displayed slight frowns of apprehension.

"It's about Rob. You remember how surprised we were when he dropped out of college and came home? His grades had been fair, and he never indicated he wanted to join me in my insurance business before.

"Well today, I may have found out why. A girl stopped in the office late today looking for Rob, but he was out. So I talked with her. She's from Bucknell. Seems to be a fine girl, claimed she was pinned by Rob and that he had talked about marriage—at least until she got pregnant. And that's when Rob packed up and came home."

Nancy's head dropped and she began massaging her forehead. Harry felt a first rush of adrenalin.

Art stared at his hands and continued. "I didn't want to believe her, but she seemed so nice. She's on her summer vacation and getting desperate. She's beginning to show and claims Rob's ignored her letters. I believe her. I thought I had better tell you right away so we can figure out how to handle this."

Nancy stared ahead. Despite their increasing estrangement, when problems arose in her life, she didn't mind standing behind Harry.

Harry was in his problem-solving mode. "Where's the girl now?"

"At the hotel in Doylestown. But she'll be back to the office or our house looking for Rob. She's not going to disappear."

It was a mess. Harry agreed. But first things first. "We're going to have to confront Rob right away and establish the truth. Based on that, we'll figure out the next step."

"How about Babs?" Nancy said archly. "I don't suppose it occurred to you to consider her wishes."

Helen sat mutely, twisting her handkerchief.

"When do you think I should discuss this with

Rob, Harry?"

"No time to lose with the girl in town. You know how fast something like this will make the rounds if it gets out. I say tonight. Rob will be bringing Babs home soon and we'll have to do it with her present."

Art nodded glumly.

As the Schoens and Hawthornes waited, the grandfather clock in the hallway loudly ticked, the only sound filling the awkward silence. Nancy had made coffee, an excuse to escape the room. Finally, the sound of a car, steps on the gravel, and a key in the lock signaled the arrival of the young couple. Their faces registered surprise to find both sets of parents waiting in the living room, at such a late hour.

"Come in and sit down," Harry instructed. Babs started to speak but Harry stopped her. The two sat close together on one of the sofas.

"Babs, honey, Mr. Hawthorne has something to resolve with Rob and it must be done now, and in front of you. Try to keep calm and we will deal with this."

Rob licked his lips quickly as his father rose and stood before him. "Ever hear of a girl named Elaine Cott, Rob?"

"Yes, I knew her at college."

"How well did you know her?"

"Oh, we dated a few times."

"Rob, she came looking for you today at the office."

Rob's eyes widened. "At the office?"

"Yes, and she'll be back. She claims you gave her your frat pin."

Babs glared at Rob and leaned away from him.

Art took a deep breath. "She also claims she's pregnant, that you're the father, and that you skipped out when she told you about the baby."

Rob hung his head. Babs's face was frozen.

"Is it true?"

"Yes," he mumbled.

Babs jumped to her feet and began to beat his head with her hands. He raised his arms to protect himself, but made no effort to fight back.

"You bastard!" she shrieked. "You lying bastard! What did you pin her with, a half-nelson? You son of a bitch!"

Harry grabbed her arms and pulled her away. "Easy honey, easy."

Harry turned to face Rob. "So you pinned her, talked about marriage, impregnated her, ran away, came here and got engaged to my daughter. Where was your head boy, up your ass?"

"I'm sorry," was all Rob could manage.

Babs, her eyes gleaming with malice, dropped her bombshell. "That's not all. The reason we were rushing with the marriage is because I think I'm pregnant."

Harry wheeled and struck Rob with an open-handed slap, so forcefully that it knocked him off the edge of the seat. Blood trickled from a nostril as Rob rested on his hands and knees on the floor.

Art jumped between Harry and Rob. "Stop Harry. I don't blame you, but please stop."

Nancy grabbed a napkin, dunked it into a water glass and quickly blotted up the drops from the rug.

Harry glared at Art, then pointed at Rob. "Get him out of here," he snarled.

"Rob, go wait in the car," Art commanded.

"No," Babs said, "he stays until this is resolved!"

Rob reclaimed his seat with a paper napkin pressed to his nose.

"Babs, do you still want him?" Harry asked.

"No," she said coldly.

"Okay, that settles it. I think you made a good decision, honey."

"Art, get your idiot son out of here. I'll take care of Babs. He and his pregnant friend are all yours. Nancy and Helen can come up with a story about incompatibility or something breaking the engagement."

"I'm sorry, Harry—really sorry. Nancy, Babs, I—."

"Just go, Art. You're a decent man. Please, just go away."

As soon as the door closed behind them, Nancy turned on Babs. "You think you're pregnant? Don't you know? Do you know what causes it, Daddy's little girl?"

Babs lifted her head. Her eyes were red and she looked like a whipped dog. "Mother, PLEASE!"

Harry stepped between them, palming the air like a referee separating a pair of boxers. "We're all upset. Let's let this lie until the morning when we can discuss it more calmly."

"I see! Since it involves your little favorite, we can ignore her lying, sneaking around, and screwing."

"Mother, you're in no position to talk!" Babs shouted as she jumped to her feet. "Why don't you tell Dad about Frenchtown?"

Nancy paled, then slapped Babs hard. The two of them stood facing each other, Babs sobbing, Nancy white and tense.

"Go ahead mother. Tell Dad about the Frenchtown Motel and the way I saw you come out of a room there and kiss John Warden. Go ahead, tell him."

"I don't have to now," Nancy hissed and walked imperiously away and up the stairs.

Babs ran from the room. Harry stood frozen for a moment, like a stunned survivor of a bomb concussion. Then he walked purposefully out the door.

Harry mashed the Warden's doorbell repeatedly until the lights finally went on and Anne Warden's worried face appeared at the pane to the side of the front door.

"Harry, what's the matter?"

"I have to see John."

"I'll get him, wait here."

Anne reappeared with John at the top of the stairs. John descended rapidly.

"Trouble Harry?"

"Yes John, for you."

"What do you mean?"

"Frenchtown."

John took a step back.

"Put 'em up, John."

"Whoa, Harry! Think for a second. It would mean a lawsuit for you."

"I don't think so, you bastard! Your father-in-law wouldn't like it."

John turned to run but Harry caught his sleeve and spun him around. John threw a wild, wide right. Harry parried with his left forearm. Drawing on lessons from his teen-age sparring at the city recreation center, he threw an inside "triple." His right hand dug deep into John's stomach. The left came off his parry, but landed too high on John's forehead. The body blow brought John's face forward and dropped his arms, leaving a huge opening for the straight right, to complete the triple.

He drove his fist into John's face, following through as though the punch was intended to stop a full foot beyond the point where it made contact. John went down hard and stayed down. Harry stepped across his prostrate body.

"Sorry Anne," he said.

"Harry," the body groaned, "tell me one thing. How am I different from you and the office wife I've heard about?"

Harry paused. "You're not. That's why I detest you." Harry left, leaving the door open.

John stirred, "Anne, Anne, help me," he said through a split lip.

She sat down next to him, cradling his head in her lap and stroking his hair. "Of course I will."

⳨ *Mox Nix*

Chapter Ten

You Can't Go Home Again

Harry was relieved to see Marie's car parked under the street light in front of her town-house on Ranstead Street. He had never before stopped without calling, but he was hurting and needed consolation. Jesus, he thought, what a streak I'm working on. The promotion had been great, but everything since has gone downhill: his career gaffe with Ernst; Charley's demotion; Nancy's involvement with that oily lawyer; and Babs's pregnancy by her profligate fiancé.

As Harry ascended the steps to her front door, he heard Marie's strident voice, answered by a man. He frowned and pushed the buzzer. The voices stopped. He pushed again.

Marie opened the door as far as the safety chain would allow. Her eyes widened. "Harry! What's.... What are you doing here?"

"I know. I should've called. But I needed to see you." He hesitated. "Of course, if you're busy."

Her explanation tumbled out. "Oh, I wish I could have you in, but Donald surprised me with a visit. He's on a training mission and his plane is laid over at McGuire for a few hours, so he borrowed a car and drove over. I'm afraid he's brought a family problem with him, but he'll be leaving in about an hour. Could you call first, and stop back?"

Harry was relieved. The male voice belonged to Marie's son. He noticed for the first time how distraught Marie was under her tightly controlled surface. Without her make-up, in the unforgiving light of the street lamp, she looked harried, haggard.

"Please, Harry."

"Of course."

He turned and started down the steps. He heard the chain lock disengaging. A male voice commanded, "Hold it. Come on in, I want to meet you."

Harry turned in time to catch Marie's fleeing back, disappearing down the hallway. He was startled by Donald's appearance—he looked a bit old to be Marie's son. Even odder, Harry had the impression, in the street light anyway, that he and Donald bore a resemblance. It was clear he had stumbled into the middle of somebody else's private nightmare. He'd had enough of his own already.

"Some other time," Harry said, turning to leave. "I've blundered into a private family matter."

"This problem concerns you too, Mr. Schoen. I think you better come in and deal with it now."

Harry's head jerked. Problem? And why is this stranger making it sound like *my* problem? He cautiously retraced his steps and entered the house, trying to steal a glance at his face.

Donald closed the door and extended his hand, with a slight grin. Harry relaxed a notch. "I'm Donald and I've heard many good things about you."

"Harry Schoen, Captain—excuse me—Major," he corrected himself, spotting the gold clusters on the open shirt collar.

"Yes. Just recently, thanks."

Harry inspected Donald and was now thoroughly struck by the similarity in their appearances. They were of similar height, build, coloring, features, and... age? Harry was forty-four. He figured Donald to be in his mid-thirties. Perhaps military life had accelerated the aging process. Long hours of extreme boredom and short minutes of extreme terror punctuated by many bouts of extreme drinking can have that effect.

Donald led the way down the hall and turned into the empty living room. "Drink?"

"Yes, Scotch will be fine."

"All out. I'm drinking V.O."

"That'll be fine."

"How do you like it?"

"Neat and large," Harry said, sighing. "This has not been one of my better days."

"Sorry to hear it. Actually this may turn out to be one of the best of my life."

Harry took a stiff quaff of the rye and stared into his glass, waiting for answers.

Donald called, "Mother dear, come out and join us."

"Donald, please don't do this," came the muffled response.

He strode to the bedroom door and opened it, "Come mother," he commanded.

Marie swept out, her face a mask of composure,

now artfully treated with cosmetics. She wore a beautiful red and black silk robe Donald had sent her from Japan the Christmas before last.

She seated herself in a winged arm chair, fumbled with a cigarette lighter, and took a deep drag, expelling the smoke too forcefully, at too steep an angle toward the ceiling.

"I'm sorry Harry," she said in a soft, even voice. You've gotten into a family quarrel. Please leave."

Harry started to rise from the couch, but Donald snapped, "Sit down Harry! This trouble belongs to you, too." Harry sagged back onto the cushion.

Fright flickered in Marie's eyes. She rose, poured herself a drink, and rustled back to her chair.

"Donald, if you do this, I'll never forgive you."

"Mother, you are the one who requires forgiveness. Forgiveness for ruining my father's life. Forgiveness for making an emotional cripple out of me. I'll live the rest of my days without forgiving myself for my failure to save my father."

His voice rose in volume, but flattened in tone. "I must do this to sever the goddamned chain of a petrified umbilical cord. It must be said, and it must be said in front of a witness, so that it doesn't get locked up in its fucking little black box and put away like it never happened, again. You're good, you're very very good at acting like things never happened, but I'm not. I know they did and I hurt."

"Harry, he's been drinking and all of this is because he wants to marry some Japanese bar girl and I don't approve. He's acting like a little boy."

Donald interrupted. "Little boy! How old you

think this little boy is Harry, old boy?"

"I'm sure I don't know."

"How about thirty-nine."

Harry blinked. Marie had made much of the fact that she was seven years older than he, but a twelve-year-old giving birth seemed implausible.

"How old are you, Harry?"

"Forty-four."

"Forty-four? That's interesting. I was told that you were fifty-two. But mother was never too good on ages."

Marie's hand trembled slightly as she raised the glass to her lips, noisily swallowing a mouthful.

"Yes, mother holds her age well, doesn't she? The best looking fifty-nine-year-old gal in town."

Marie lowered her eyes, then looked straight at Harry.

"I did say I was too old for you." A faint note of apology had entered her voice. "I had to lie about it to get my job at Schopfer years ago, and I just let it ride. I'm sorry."

All Harry could do was nod numbly.

"Mother is upset about me marrying a bar girl. In fact, I am marrying a lovely, university-educated Japanese girl, whose family has reluctantly accepted me. But it wouldn't matter if she were a princess. Mother dear doesn't want me to marry, period!" He looked at Harry, "Ever think about why an attractive woman such as she didn't re-marry?"

Harry managed a limp "No."

"Did she ever tell you about my father's death?"

Marie started sobbing, the type of sob which is

restrained until it bursts forth, akin to an emotional hiccup. "No Donald. Don't, please."

"I guess you were too busy enjoying yourself and discharging your own demons, Harry old boy, to ever think deeply about MaMa," Donald sneered.

"Well, MaMa drove PaPa to suicide."

Marie was now crying softly.

"When he came to understand that my mother cared for me, and only me, in all ways, he couldn't handle it. He drank more and more and worked less and less. And then one night, when I was home from college in my senior year, I heard him lay it all out for her. I was in my room, but I opened the door to hear, and did I hear!"

Donald's eyes opened wide and his face had gone pale with anger. He stood over Marie who now huddled, holding her arms crossed, like someone who has been punched hard in the belly, crying softly. The tears started as dark mascara rivulets, but were muddied by the pancake as they descended.

Donald now paced the room as he went on with his soliloquy. "For the first time, I allowed myself to understand the bathrobes that would fall open, the many times when I was the slightest bit ill; that mommy would sleep with me instead of my father, the way that she would bring my shirt to me when I was still in the shower, and the enemas. Oh Christ, the enemas. I was a most regular little boy! All of the girls who were welcomed by mother, but then would have their faults so artfully analyzed and pointed out for me."

Harry lowered his head and stared into his drink

as Donald moved woodenly across the room and slumped into a chair.

All of the emotion in his voice and eyes was gone as he droned on. "That night as I eavesdropped, I noticed that my father was fully sober for the first time in a long time. I think he was trying to save me. By that time he was a weak man, his balls had been taken off a long time before, snip by snip by mother, but he still tried. He pleaded with mother to let me go, to recognize what a sick relationship the three of us had descended into.

"But as usual, strong, reliable, confident, and utterly wrong, mother denied everything. She mocked him and his 'evil mind.' She belittled his manhood. I have never heard such devastatingly cruel insults.

"He left the house. I looked out my bedroom window as he slowly walked to his car. I wanted to go to him but I didn't. He looked back once and slowly drove away. About a half hour later, the police came and said that he must have been drunk. They had seen him that way many times. On a straight, wide highway, he suddenly veered off and smashed into a bridge abutment at seventy miles an hour. There were no skid marks."

Donald took a sip of his drink.

"As soon as I graduated from college and turned twenty-one, I signed a recruiting contract and escaped into the service. Even mother couldn't interfere with the Air Force, although for a time she tried to follow me from base to base, before she gave up.

Harry's mind was spinning from all the crazy revelations he'd been privy to, all in one night.

"For eighteen years I have been trying to forget

that I didn't go to my father that night. I have been trying to establish a normal relationship with a woman, and by God I finally have, and I'm going to marry her, I'm going to be a complete man."

He rose. Dark circles had bloomed in the armpits of his blouse. He belted the rest of his drink.

It was quiet. It was still.

Donald walked to the closet and pulled out his uniform jacket, buttoning it slowly. He took his hat in his hand and walked to his mother's side. "I'm sorry, mother, but it had to be done." He patted her on the shoulder and one of her hands quickly rose to meet his. He peeled her grasping fingers from his wrist and walked out.

The sound of the door closing broke the spell. Harry moved to her side and awkwardly put his arm around her shoulder, but instead of turning her head into his shoulder, she pushed it away.

"Go away, Harry."

"I love you, and I want to help you."

"Go away, Harry."

He rose. "I'll call you in the morning."

"No."

"I will."

"No. Don't. Please don't."

Harry let himself out and trudged to his car. He sat behind the wheel, trying to make sense of the wreckage. He and Marie now understood the true nature of what had seemed to be a soul-mate love affair. They had used each other, Marie to relieve her long repressed incestuous desires for Donald, and Harry to release the tensions of his rigidly-controlled corporate life and cold marriage.

His enjoyment of her unbridled lust for him was now just a soiled memory. Her passion had been expended *with* him, but had not been *for* him. He now realized that while Marie's bed had only two occupants, he had not been one. For the first time in his life, Harry Schoen had no place to go. Automatically, he glanced at his watch.

Somehow Harry's car took him home, like the faithful horse that returns to its stall. That night, he drank himself into a stupor with his good friend, Crown Royal. This friend had often provided succor. When he drank heavily, which was rare, his mind escaped from its cage of rationality and logic. It would soar, and sometimes crash.

He started out with his Germanic obsession with the misuse and disuse of time. He reflected on the great amount of his time which had slipped away while he wasn't looking. He realized for the first time that he was on the down slope side of his personal mountain. Another swig of ethanol and he moved along to considering his relationships with others, including God. Inevitably he considered his own death in light of the way he was wasting his time. His ramble staggered along this way:

Time, time, time. What makes time so damn important? A man who frequently checks his watch on the coast-to-coast jet—looks at watch—where the hell is he going, going to get off? No, he is stuck like all the others. But look at that watch. Is he anxious for time to pass, pass, pass. WHY? Does he want to die because that is all time represents? Or is it? No, time equals hope, and that is what we poor slobs live on—spend all our fucking lives waiting for time to go by because next year we are really going to live it up.

Travel? Shit, we'll go to Disneyland and blow the roll. When I'm ready to die, I'll really be ready to live. My annuity at sixty-five will allow me to pay all my medical bills and make that commercialized humanitarian doctor rich, rich, rich. Don't get your fatal illness on Wednesday—doctor golfs. When I'm old and gray, I'll be financially able to do all the things I can physically and mentally do when I'm young and brown. "I want to live not die, I wanna laugh not cry." That's what the song says, but what do we really do with time? Mostly we observe it and wait for it to pass, and does it pass, baby.

Some slide through life on the track of alcohol and/or tranquilizers while their "psycho" analysts help them cop out on their parents for two hundred bucks an hour with their friction-reducing balms. But without friction, no heat is generated. Without heat there is no warmth. Imagine a perfect lubricant for the penis—stroke effortlessly, without reaction, sensation, or irritation to be relieved.

Male and female, individual and society, man and God can make their lubricants so perfect that they cease to note the existence of one another. Cogito ergo sum, Cogito ergo come, Cuma sum laude, cuma sum loudly—Lordy—or don't bother to come at all.

Chapter Eleven

The Mice Come Home To Roost

The rest of the summer passed uneventfully. As winter approached, Harry sought refuge from the shambles of his personal life by plunging deeper into his work. Marie quit and moved to Florida, refusing to the last to see Harry, her pseudo-son-lover, outside of their rigid office encounters. He did receive a short note when she left, thanking him for the good times but concluding that a love affair was like a thoroughbred race horse. When it breaks a leg, the kindest thing is to shoot it.

Charley Winston was an occasional voice on the telephone. Harry had shot him, too. Babs missed a period but was not pregnant after all. Rob moved to Elaine's home town in the western part of the state, married her and went to work in her father's small metal-working mill. He would, like an electric current, always follow the path of least resistance, or like water, always run downhill.

Babs had explained to Harry that she was the winner and Elaine became the loser when she had "won" Rob. Harry agreed with her new-found, or newly revealed, wisdom. Babs had decided to go away to school, not to seek education, but to obtain degrees, socialize, and avoid her parents and friends.

Nancy and Harry continued to exist in the same house, but they rarely spoke and when they did, certainly said nothing. Why they maintained the facade of marriage was an interesting question which neither of them cared to examine. Mutual guilt over their moribund affairs exerted the powerful force of inertia. "Moving bodies or bodies at rest tend to remain in motion or at rest" is also true for people. The shell was maintained so Babs would have a place to come to during college breaks.

Of course, there were the social appearances which made their marriage convenient for both. Harry attended Nancy's club functions, and Nancy appeared on Harry's arm at his business-related social affairs. They now lived celibate lives. The only oasis of normalcy was their daughter Ellen, who somehow managed to have a happy marriage with her conventional husband and darling baby boy. Harry and Nancy both delighted in the child, but separately.

Charley Bothswel, the VP for Marketing, was amazed by Harry's industry and productivity. He read it as Harry's desire to cement himself in a position to succeed him as VP for Marketing next year, when he retired. He reported Harry's fine work to Ernst, who read it as an effort by Harry to recoup his position after his gaffe in supporting Robert's attempt to mitigate Ernst's harsh "BOB" program.

Both were wrong. The work was Harry's salvation and his passion, which now had no other outlet. He did not drive himself. He simply had no other interest in his life beyond his career. He rose, went to work, labored until deeply tired, and went home to sleep. His subordinates could not keep up with him and shook their heads in disbelief as he revealed deeply detailed knowledge of all their individual specialized projects. He was a dynamo.

The "Boosting our Business" Program had been completely put into effect, leaving a shocked, demoralized, and sullen corporation in its wake. The senior employees had played by the rules, only to discover that in mid-game, the company changed the rules. Of course, Wall Street analysts applauded the efforts to make Schopfer Chemical "lean and mean." Company profits rose, not from real growth, but because of the general economic recovery, combined with the reduction in payroll.

Harry's new intern from Wharton was a very bright young black man, long on street smarts and short on social grace. Looking over his transcripts, it was clear that he never would have gotten into Penn Undergrad or the Wharton Graduate School, except as a special project. Harry took an instant liking to him based on his candor and hard work. As with a number of blacks, he had an Irish name, Tyrone McDuffy, a likely throw back to the many Irish planters of the old South.

Tyrone, the son of a funeral director, understood fierce competition, and the need to cover bases. His father was a member of the Masons, Lions, Elks, NAACP, Rotary, VFW, Chamber of Commerce, sang in the choir of one church, belonged to a Bible study group at a second, and attended evening services at a third. He appreciated the sacrifices his parents had made to steer him and his siblings through the mean streets of North Philadelphia to careers in nursing, pharmacy, law, and business.

Harry gave him several market research projects involved in finding additional uses for technology developed for a specific market segment, and examining market segments that Schopfer was not involved in to assess their suitability and possible entry points. These projects brought him into contact with many disciplines within and without the corporation, but called for independent analysis, conclusions, and recommendations. They ended with a formal presentation to a varied audience at the firm, who could then consider the merits of the research and the researcher.

Harry served as his mentor and critic, but far more as a sounding board. He did not so much guide him as drop a couple of bread crumbs indicating a possible route. They had frequent lunches at the In-Towner Club to discuss his projects. Harry discovered that he enjoyed being a mentor to Tyrone. It provided some relief from his own barren life.

Tyrone was an eager pupil who thirsted for Harry's knowledge. He also carefully instructed him in proper "corporate speak" and corporate protocol. The former was easy, how to select words and phrases to secure the best reaction. There is a general corporate speak and a specialized version for each company, and Harry was expert in both. As a line manager, many times he had to tell staff people and executives things they did not want to hear.

The second was a more difficult topic, but Harry

found a way. "Tyrone, I'm going to raise a topic with you that you may think is trivial and likely will anger you, but I'll ask you to consider my motivation for doing so. Do you really think that I'm going to waste my time on minutiae or that I am seeking another enemy?

"I assure you I have more than I need. So here goes—you have got to work on your table manners. For instance, you make a slurping noise when you drink. I know that sounds trivial, but do that with high level people and many of them will tune out every thing you say thereafter.

"You don't have to read Emily Post, but go slow and observe the people you are with and do as they do. You're going to see place settings with more instruments than any sane person needs. Do you really need a special fork to eat an oyster, or a fish knife, or a finger bowl? No, but these are all part of a special code that opens doors for you."

Tyrone took it rather well, Harry thought. Likely better than he would have himself.

He also explained that business is like trying to go up the down escalator: if you stand still, you end up on your ass on the floor below; if you jog, you go nowhere. You have got to run to get to the next level.

Harry hoped that this sort of tutoring was going on throughout the firm now that the ideal job applicant at Schopfer was a black female with a Spanish surname and one eye. She could be counted four times against the equal employment objectives. Line managers were forced to accept unqualified minority employees and tutor and lubricate them into equal pay slots, frequently resented by long-term employees. But the

Board of Directors approached its own Equal Employment Opportunity obligation cautiously, recruiting a woman who was a vice president of a prestigious business consulting firm, and an outstanding successful black businessman. Such was their contribution.

And then the shit began to hit the fan. An editor from the *Philadelphia Times* called Ernst to tell him he was working on a story about health and safety issues at Schopfer which he felt obligated to report, but wished to inform Ernst in advance and give him a chance to comment. Days later, two investigative reporters arrived for an audience with Ernst, Joe Graber, Allen Higgins, the legal VP, and Dr. Bellington, the VP for Research and Corporate Health. Ernst felt uneasy about press relations and the possibility of unfavorable publicity, but speculated that this was likely just another case of old Schopfer chemical drums turning up in a landfill somewhere.

The newsmen made a strange pairing. The larger and older man was much larger, and introduced himself as Willis Brophy. Unruly hair, with a thick mustache below, formed a mane about his ruddy and rutted face. His suit was rumpled and a large belly forced his belt into a low arc. He smiled easily and spoke in a soft and rather friendly voice.

Willis Brophy had grown up fatherless in the City of Brotherly Love, at Girard College, a school and home for fatherless boys endowed by Stephen Girard, a merchant prince of the past. There he played soccer, a religion at the school, and through it met members of all of the European ethnic groups that competed at the old Lighthouse Field Club.

He had access to all of the Irish, German, Italian, Ukranian, Hispanic, Hungarian, Polish, and Jewish enclaves in the city. This allowed Willis to know the police, union officials, stevedores, gangsters, judges, restaurateurs, politicians, priests, rabbis, and ministers of the row house work-a-day sections of the city. They trusted and wanted to help him, as he could always be counted on to intercede for a friend in trouble, get some publicity for the church bazaar, introduce an athlete to a college coach, listen sympathetically, buy a drink, or dispense an unseen five-dollar bill.

Willis had many ears and eyes for his sharp brain. This, added to his own unique nose for things that did not smell right, and the magical Irish ability to craft words, made him formidable.

The other reporter was much younger and neater, small and birdlike. His motions were as abrupt as his comments. His hair was black, his face clean shaven, although the dark whiskers beneath his skin gave his face a bluish tint. His voice was shrill and all sentences, even declarative, ended with a slight rise in tone which caused people to respond to them as questions.

The group exchanged banalities for a few moments until Ernst launched the meeting by telling the reporters he was sure they were busy people. He then explained the functions of the executives who were present and asked the reporters how he could be of service.

Brophy smiled pleasantly and began.

"Gentlemen, my colleague and I are investigative reporters. About six months ago, our paper was approached with a possible story involving some very serious allegations about health problems involving your firm. We were quite dubious, but we have now completed a thorough investigation and have reluctantly come to the conclusion that the charges appear valid and worthy of printing." His smile had disappeared.

"What are these 'allegations?'" Ernst inquired. Like a cat feigning indifference, he became occupied with the unwrapping of a cigar.

Brophy responded in a voice that made a miraculous transition from casually genial to sharply chiseled. "That your firm negligently exposed workers at your Philadelphia plant to a carcinogenic chemical back in the late 1950s and early 1960s."

"That's preposterous," Dr. Bellington sputtered. "What a scurrilous accusation to—."

Higgins cut him off.

"These men are here doing their professional duties. Let's hear them out." He then addressed Brophy directly. "You, of course, must fully appreciate the seriousness and the consequences of your statements." He put just a shading of accent on the word consequences.

"Yes sir, I do. Our editor specifically wanted us to advise you of our findings prior to publication to provide you with an opportunity to respond."

"What are the details?" asked Graber. When the words "carcinogenic chemical" were spoken, Ernst had tried to hide his panic by fumbling with lighting his cigar. He understood the reason for Bellington's outburst.

"The allegations are that your firm became aware

that a chemical used in one of your processes at the Philadelphia plant was a carcinogen and that you did not properly warn your production workers. The timing of this event was 1958 to 1960. The chemical was dibromomethyl ether. As a result of the exposure, seven men contracted lung cancer and have since died. We have also learned that your firm refused to accept early warnings, based on skin testing with mice, despite pleas from cancer researchers."

Ernst now looked at Brophy and asked incredulously, "You really don't plan to use such a tragic event to sell newspapers, do you? I can't believe...." His voice trailed off.

Higgins stepped into the void. "Gentlemen, when do you plan to print the story?"

"In the Sunday edition, two weeks from now," chirped the bird.

"Why, that only gives us ten days to examine your copy and comment!"

"Beg your pardon, sir" began Brophy, "but I write under my own by-line and only my editor criticizes my work before it is published."

"I suggest then that you give me your editor's name."

"John Gallino" he said, writing on his note pad the name and number. He tore off the page and laid it on the table.

"Good day, gentlemen," he said. "Call me if you have anything to say."

Sparrow hopped out behind him and could not resist turning for a final sneering smile.

The door clicked closed. Higgins turned to

Ernst.

"I thought I knew all about this Ernst. Do I?"

Ernst sighed heavily.

Bellington fidgeted with his tie. Graber had been financial manager of the Bridesburg plant throughout much of the time period of Brophy's interest, before he had been posted to Europe. He sat and looked out the window. Higgins remained silent, but intent.

"It started years ago at our Philadelphia plant," Ernst began. "The medical doctor there recorded two cases of lung cancer, of a rare type, about a year apart. At his suggestion, we called in the National Health Institute. They went over our health records and said the cases were not statistically significant. A year later, there were two more. An internal study determined that all of the men had worked in the same manufacturing process. We checked all of the materials involved, but none was considered to be a carcinogen.

"Nonetheless, we closed up the process, put in new ventilating systems, and still had three more cases a year later. We informed the government of our findings, and alerted other firms who produced or used the chemical. We started cancer testing programs with expert laboratories.

"We then went back and designed a fully automated, bottled-up process where operators remained outside the production area. We also installed automated detection and alarm systems, and had no problems for years.

"The seven men all died. However, two more cases have turned up recently. Likely the disease has a long induction period, and people exposed before the process improvements are still at risk."

Higgins was the first to speak. "It is a tragic story, but it doesn't sound like the firm was negligent. The problem seems to be that you didn't go public with the story, so now it will be made to look like a conspiracy. I recommend that we get a copy of the article, use our outside legal firm to depose witnesses, and construct a case for internal review. After this, we'll prepare a press release and schedule a press conference."

Ernst nodded and asked if this could be done before the article was published, hopefully adding that the paper might even drop the article when the editors knew the full story.

"Not likely at all," said Higgins. "This is too juicy to pass up. But at least we'll be prepared to make our side public. Who is the most knowledgeable person to handle this?"

"That would be me," Dr. Bellington proclaimed.

———•—•———

In eight days—lightning speed for a corporation—a press conference was called and a release was ready to send to news agencies. Willis Brophy entered the conference room for the press briefing at a languid pace. He slowly pushed his shapeless Stetson hat back on his head, allowing some unkempt salt and pepper hair to dangle over his forehead and watery eyes. He gazed about the room giving barely perceptible nods or winks to fellow reporters from the various city sheets. In the pecking order of Philadelphia papers, his ranked third behind the staid, establishment, main line, Republican *Evening Standard* with its smug motto, "In Philadelphia, nearly everyone reads the *Standard*." "Nearly everyone" was to be translated as "everyone who is somebody."

Next came the *Morning Enquirer*, which played more to a blue collar, Democratic constituency. Their staff tended to view themselves as liberal keepers of the flame of democracy and featured exposes based on investigative reporting. In reality, most people bought it because it was the only morning paper, and had the overnight sports scores.

Willis's paper, *The Daily Times*, was looked down upon by peers and superiors as a "three S sheet"—sex, sensationalism and sports. The latter consumed almost half of the paper and covered everything from horse races to local high school events. In truth, some of its columnists were quite good, but tended to be obscured by front page photographs of murder victims and blaring headlines. Willis was one of the good columnists with a sharp tough mind masked by a rumpled appearance. As such, he was afforded a modicum of recognition from his competitors.

Bobby asked Harry to attend so he could report his personal reaction to the press conference. Harry had misgivings on the choice of Bellington as spokesman. While he had dealt with the medical community on the problem and looked more like an executive than anyone else at Schopfer, Harry regarded Bellington as arrogant, autocratic, and aloof. However, if Bellington stuck to the script that Harry had read, and kept it short and simple, it would go all right.

The script was written under the "KISS" formula, "Keep It Simple Stupid." It contained a statement expressing the deeply felt shock and sadness of all company employees, gave a brief chronology of the events, emphasized that the firm itself called the National Health Institute at a very early date, as soon as the company doctor observed a second case of a rare type of lung cancer. Despite the N.I.H. statement, the company then launched its own investigation, improving the process.

The company noted the publication of a shocking report that a prominent researcher at Mount Hood Hospital, with whom Dr. Bellington had consulted at an early date, had independently examined the problem. He discovered that while the base chemicals were not carcinogens, one, *mono*bromomethyl ether, contained a minute quantity of a differing chemical structure, *di*bromomethyl ether. That was a potent carcinogen—so potent that even miniscule levels of one part in one hundred million parts of air were dangerous, roughly equivalent to a teaspoon of water in an Olympic swimming pool. These levels were likely exceeded, despite the prior efforts of the company to minimize worker exposure.

At this point the company voluntarily ceased production to ensure worker safety. Now armed with the new knowledge of the specific chemical structure, a new, even tighter process was adopted, with automatic monitoring and alarm systems, and space suiting of the workers. This solved the problem and allowed production to resume.

All of this information was freely shared with

the government, competitive firms who made similar products, and with the workers themselves. However, regrettably, as with some things such as smoking, it was now apparent that there was an induction period and workers who had been exposed under the old conditions began to develop the fatal lung cancer. There was nothing that could be done but maintain a death watch and grieve as each new victim was diagnosed and began his journey toward the grave.

The statement then noted that Schopfer had always been an ethical firm with one of the best safety records in the industry, and extremely high worker loyalty. This sorrowful event was felt by the firm and its employees as a family tragedy.

Bellington closed by noting that additional press bulletins would be issued in the future and that he had no other information or comments to make at this time.

Harry had other misgivings about the event, aside from Bellington himself. Harry had taken a public relations course in business school and, as usual for him, remembered the four basic rules for a firm to follow if it has a problem:

1. Always have a professional P.R. person.

2. If you are dumb enough not to have a pro, only let one company executive speak with the press.

3. Never, never, never let more than one company representative speak with the press.

4. If you have a problem, quickly gather the facts and call a press conference and prepare a press release, before the press itself ferrets out the story.

The Schopfer Corporation had already broken

two of the four rules, and it would move on to make it all four. Since Schopfer did not manufacture any products directly for consumers, but rather sold to other firms who used its products in formulating a myriad of products, they did not have a public relations department. Unlike DuPont, who hung nylon tags on carpets, or Dow with their oven cleaners, or Union Carbide with their batteries and anti-freeze, Schopfer's products were unknown to consumers.

Also, because its stock was narrowly held by institutional investors who wanted direct access to company executives rather than to read press releases, it rarely issued them. The company was unprepared for the transition to modern times when consumerism would play a big role beyond the basic needs of a job to provide food, clothing and shelter.

Schopfer still believed, naively, that providing secure, fair wage employment with excellent benefits and pensions, being involved in civic projects, paying dividends to stockholders, and taxes to governments was all that was required.

Secondly, the firm had not notified the press to announce the problem. Instead, the press had learned of the situation independently and now the company was reacting to it.

As the stated time arrived, a door at the front of the room opened and Dr. Bellington emerged, preceded by Bleischift, the head of the Schopfer's Advertising Department, which handled public relations as an after-thought. Bellington looked calm and serious, but Bleischift looked startled and blinked owlishly as the TV lights from the local stations washed away all shadows.

"Thank you for attending, gentlemen," Mr. Bleis-chift began in a reedy voice, rushing to add "and ladies," acknowledging the women in attendance.

"As you likely have heard, we have had a dismay-ing problem at our Philadelphia plant and we have asked you here today so that we can inform you of the facts. Dr. Wallace Bellington, Senior VP of Research for Schopfer Chemical, will make the statement," Bleischift said, as he extended his arm to shift atten-tion toward Bellington and away from himself. He was relieved that all eyes, including the cycloptic red eyes of the TV cameras, turned to Bellington as he took the podium.

Bellington looked regal and pained as he followed the script with little reference to his notes. He spoke in a full patrician voice, which conveyed the crushing sadness the deaths of the plant workers caused the Schopfer family.

Harry began to breathe again as Bellington approached the end of the statement. It had been a flawless performance. His normally imperious tone and words were not apparent. He finished, thanked those assembled, noted that there would be another press conference as more information became avail-able, and started to turn as Bleischift moved to the exit door and held it open for his departure.

The reporters began to clamor with questions as Bellington sought to stay them by raising his hands and motioning for quiet. "There really isn't any more to say at this time. However, if you will submit your questions in written form, I will respond directly to you. Thank you."

He again turned to leave when Brophy's voice boomed through the crowd, "Hey Mister Bellington! I hear that there are more cases than you said. Which number's the right one?"

Bellington turned back from the door and fixed Brophy with a glare. With a small smile he said with a distinct note of irritation, "My name is Doctor Bellington."

Ouch! thought Harry. Just say, "I have no more comments at this time" and exit, PLEASE!

Brophy now had a harpoon in as he archly said, "Excuse me, I didn't know you were a medical man."

Bellington explained that those with Ph.D.'s are referred to as Doctor too. His patronizing tones and manners began to show.

Brophy now changed the pace as he bored in, "Look, Bellington, the question was about the number of dying men, not about titles. You accounted for nine in your statement but a little bird told me that two more men have just shown some suspicious spots on their X-rays last week and the correct number should be eleven!"

Oh, God, here it goes down the tube, Harry thought as he felt his breathing slow.

"I told you the number," Bellington coldly hissed, and then strode imperiously out the door. The TV cameras continued to shoot. Harry knew that was the image they'd use on the evening newscasts.

✠

Chapter Twelve

Into the Pit and a Thread to Climb

T he winter of misery dragged on. Body after body fell ill with the same rare form of lung cancer, dying soon thereafter. The death count was now eleven. Schopfer Chemical was being murdered by the media. The tragedy had been mishandled from the beginning. The company had now broken each of the four rules for public relations for dealing with the problem, including permitting multiple executives to speak with the press. This allowed reporters to drive wedges into the cracks between the separate statements.

Under the twin loads of the deaths and the demoralizing impact of the "BOB" Program (now called "BOOB" by the employees), company morale plummeted to new lows.

The tragedy made fodder for a muck-raking book, and television investigative reports. To compound the problem, Lorraine Zdanowski, whose father had been one of the early victims, formed a loose group of the workers and survivors to press the company for a concrete program of aid, ongoing information, and compensation. It was she who had first alerted newsman Willis Brophy, and now stirred the pot regularly. The slow moving, normally secretive company, now paralyzed by fear and acting only by consensus in the absence of a strong leader, stumbled about, mumbling platitudes.

Ernst and Graber finally realized they needed a skilled negotiator to deal directly with Miss Zdanowski and her group. While discussing the problem with Ernst and Graber, Bobby proposed Harry's name, citing his skill in fashioning contracts with major customers, and the high esteem in which he was held by subordinates. Ernst seized on the idea, remembering how determined Harry was about making his next promotion, and how easily and completely he had yielded to the "BOB" plan.

Harry was informed that he was to drop all his present duties immediately, and devote all of his energies to "bringing the problem under control." Ernst noted that he would be personally grateful if Harry could make quick order of the mess. Harry was dismayed to have to catch a hot potato with both hands, but accepted the assignment with his usual "Yes sir."

Harry began by securing copies of all company and newspaper files on the topic, reading the exposé book on the event, and watching tapes of the TV news and interview shows. He read medical texts on the rare form of cancer involved and reports on all the toxicity testing.

The next step was a series of interviews with all company employees with any involvement, starting with Dr. Bellington, and progressing through the plant doctor who first flagged the problem, the plant manager, area manager, shift leaders, and plant operators who were directly involved. He constructed a dismayingly long chronology of events and examined decisions from a "what if?" view.

Harry discovered that it had taken years to make improvements in the process, equipment, and industrial hygiene. He concluded that the company had not actively managed the problem but had reactively wandered through it. During this time the ion-exchange resin product line based on the hazardous chemicals proved to be a major technical improvement, used in filtering water to yield the extremely high purity water required for production of flawless microchips for computers. Its sales volumes and profits became important to this corporation.

Harry's initial impression left him with a mixed bag. Yes, the company was quick to report suspicious deaths, but based on statistical assurance, took no action until further deaths. To its credit, even after being told the deaths were still not statistically significant, Schopfer contacted a premier medical center in New York and began negotiations for testing of raw materials used in the building where the two deceased men had worked.

However, Harry was appalled to learn from the operators in the building that an exothermic reaction during the production process often led to the expulsion of hot noxious choking gases which they, with characteristic bravado, ignored. Harry remembered his own college lab work, always done in a hood that carried gases away, and the rejoinder of his old organic chemistry professor: "If it ain't air, don't breathe it." The process should have been adjusted to control the fumes, and better exhaust provided as a back up, as was now the case, plus positive draft helmets for the men.

The former two steps should have been done as early as possible as a routine part of good industrial hygiene, without waiting for health problems to appear. Harry determined that none of the research chemists who had worked carefully with the materials had been afflicted. This pointed him toward the conclusion that a sloppy production process was the cause. Harry's confidence in the company's position on the topic was beginning to wane.

He was also puzzled by the fact that a testing contract with the premiere Mount Hood Hospital cancer researcher had never been executed, but three months later was contracted out to another, less-qualified organization. He pursued the topic with Dr. Bellington, who declared that the first doctor "was abrasive, and insisted on the right to publish his work."

"I see," Harry replied, thinking, *What a dumb answer.* Who cares if the medical researcher wasn't lovable, if he was the best man to examine the problem? Besides, abrasiveness toward Bellington might mean that the researcher had asked some pointed questions or failed to properly pay homage to Bellington's great intellect. Also, why bother to object to printing the results? If the cause was not identified, there would be no problems with that. If it was identified, Schopfer would be obligated to print it for the common good!

Harry asked Bellington when he was convinced the cancers were directly related to the process. The inane response was, when epidemiological data confirmed it. Who needed additional data when mouse skin tests had pointed that way and when bodies were falling, all with the same rare form of cancer!

The cancer researchers had pleaded with the company to accept the validity of the mouse skin tests, but the company resisted until they were confirmed by inhalation tests with mice. The inhalation test results with mice were shockingly bad. They predicted a tolerance level of only one part of dibromomethylether in one hundred million parts of air. Even then, Schopfer officials continued to question the validity of animal tests and insisted that epidemiology data were needed to prove the link with human cancers.

It struck Harry that epidemiology had been employed by the company the way a political scoundrel wraps himself in the flag to prove he is a patriot. Likewise, a firm which has done a poor job on industrial hygiene and ignored warning signs of toxicity problems can decide at the end to run such a study and claim that it is the only "statistically scientific" way to examine the problem.

Harry believed, in light of the standard of knowledge of the time, that the firm had acted in good faith, but far too slowly.

Now that Harry possessed his own knowledge of the situation, he moved on to deal with the people problems. He called the Philadelphia plant manager's office and got Lorraine Zdanowski. He explained who he was, his mission, and asked her to join him for lunch near the plant to discuss her concerns. She was polite, but told Harry she had already met with a number of company officials.

"Yes, but I am the one who is going to resolve the problems."

When she entered the small dining room adjacent to the bar, he was struck by her appearance: tall, slim, attractive, mid-twenties. She saw him and strode positively to the table, stuck out her hand to shake, and quickly seated herself. She had piercing green eyes that looked straight into his. "Drink?"

"Sure." Lorraine turned her head and hailed a waitress. "Stella, Old Grand Dad on the rocks for me, and whatever this fellow wants."

"Make it two," Harry added, following his salesman's automatic approach of liking whatever the customer likes.

They talked as they ate their kielbasa and sauerkraut platters. He quickly got the message that you did not chat with Zdanowski, you spoke directly and you answered questions directly. "What do you want or need?" Harry asked.

"Straight prompt answers to questions, to be kept informed of all medical results, to be assured that all medical bills are covered and processed by the company, not the families, that financial aid be given to all affected workers—alive or dead. That if any special needs arise for the families because of the illnesses they are taken care of pronto, and the agreement that none of these actions have any bearing on any future legal actions or settlements."

Harry looked directly into her face, extended his hand across the table and said, "Done." Her eyes gave one quick blink but she returned his firm hand shake.

"Now, I have a request. I want to meet with your group, and I want them to be prepared to detail every last complaint and concern they have. I want to do this without reporters or lawyers present, and I will come by myself."

She sat back for a moment and then said, "Agreed. My house, Wednesday night, seven o'clock." She took a small notepad from her pocketbook, scribbled her address and phone number, said thanks for the lunch, wheeled and strode out the door.

When Harry reported orally to the top company management team (he had decided to put nothing in writing or in company files on this problem), he was greeted with frowns and chair shuffling, particularly when he made the proposal that supplemental paychecks be extended to all affected men and their families to cover their pressing needs while settlement negotiations were pursued. This gesture was intended for goodwill even though it might reduce the pressure on the men to settle rapidly.

A few pointed questions and some "helpful" suggestions followed. As usual, these senior executives were far more active critics than action people. Harry parried and answered politely for a time, until he finally spoke with emphasis saying, "Look, I did not start with a level playing field, but from the depths of a great hole I'm trying to climb out of."

Ernst stepped in. "Harry has to be given a great deal of latitude, up to the point where financial settlements are discussed." Of course all negative tones were instantly replaced with reinforcing votes of confidence.

The meeting closed with Higgins, the head of legal, saying that there was to be no report of the meeting and that attendees should destroy their notes. He also stated, "Harry's move in getting the workers' families to accept money in addition to their worker's compensation is a highly desirable low-cost way to reduce hostility and likely facilitate less acrimonious negotiations, and improve public relations."

———·•·———

Harry arrived at Lorraine's house at exactly seven. He left the new Cadillac coupe at home and drove the six-year-old Chevy station wagon, bearing a couple of small dents and scratches. He dressed neatly but down—to a navy blazer and camel slacks, with his early evening chin stubble.

He made his way through the gate of the low wrought-iron fence that surrounded the small front lawn, and up the three steps to the wooden, roofed, front porch. Harry pushed the doorbell. The door swung open to reveal an unsmiling, but polite, Lorraine. She invited him into a small dark foyer.

Stairs rose to the second floor and next to them a

hallway led past a living room with flowered slip covers on stuffed furniture, a small TV set, and a crucifix displayed prominently on the wall. Next was a small dining room with a dark oak table and chairs, and a china cabinet.

Finally, they entered a large, brightly lit kitchen that spanned the width of the house and extended into a pantry with a sloping roof that had been added to the rear of the original house. Seated around the table were five middle-aged men and two women. The men were drinking beers, in some cases as chasers for straight shots of rye from a bottle of "Old Philadelphia" sitting on the table. The women sat next to each other sipping coffee.

Lorraine introduced Harry to the group, most of whom had Polish names, with one German and one Irish in the mix. The greetings were mostly subdued nods although one beefy fellow in a plaid flannel shirt thrust his hand out to offer a firm handshake. The men were all chemical operators from the plant. The women were widows of their deceased colleagues.

Lorraine directed Harry to an empty chair. He accepted a beer, declining a glass to drink from the bottle, as were the other men. Harry removed his blazer and hung it on the chair back, loosened his tie and collar, and was seated. Lorraine gave a brief introduction: Harry's title, years with the company, and a recount of their lunch meeting.

Harry spoke briefly. "I'm here to express the deep grief of the Schopfer family and tell you that Ernst and Robert have specifically directed me to do whatever is necessary to aid the victims and their families. That is why I asked Lorraine to arrange this meeting: I want to learn about your specific problems so that I can help you."

Silence. Harry patiently waited. Finally, Plaid Shirt said, "That sounds good. But how come it's taking so long for Workmen's Compensation checks to get started?"

"That's a function of the state government's slowness in processing claims, but based on my conversation with Miss Zdanowski, I have authorized supplemental paychecks which have already been mailed to all the affected people. When combined with the Workers Compensation checks, the total will equal the amount workers were paid for a normal forty-hour work week.

"I hate to say it, but it's true: trust me, the checks are in the mail. I stopped at payroll before I came here, and they all went out today. They will continue to arrive each week, until this entire tragedy is resolved."

A widow piped up testily, "I'm behind on my mortgage."

Harry pulled one of his business cards from his shirt pocket and slid it across the table. "Here's a card with my phone number. The back paychecks you will receive in a day or two should handle it. If not, call me, and I will."

A man interjected, "How come nobody tells us what the hell the laboratory tests showed?"

"I'll tell you right now," Harry said. "I studied them intensely, and they are not good. What they showed was that the base material, *mono*bromomethyl ether, shows a very low level of carcinogenic activity, which was new information. I read the toxicity data on the chemical that was in the literature prior to this, and it wasn't considered bad. So the way it was handled with the early process improvements should have reduced exposure to a harmless level."

Harry shifted in his chair and his voice softened as he continued, "Unfortunately, we then learned something worse. The base chemical contains a low level of *di*bromomethyl ether, and it is nasty. As soon as animal inhalation testing showed that the dibromomethyl ether was strongly toxic, the plant was closed down for spacesuiting. This was done in spite of the fact that, at that time, the validity of mouse testing correlating with humans was not readily accepted, especially since the mice used in the tests are bred to be cancer prone."

Harry paused, allowing that news to be digested before proceeding. "Later, the first evidence began to be shown in sacrificed mice that some cell changes started to show in their lungs." Harry sighed. "Unfortunately, it went on to produce lung cancers in mice. It was a different form of cancer from what our workers had, but it was still cancer. We responded as fast as possible. However, there is an induction period after exposure, like cigarette smoking, where it can take twenty to thirty years for the problem to appear in some smokers, and never in others."

Plaid Shirt asked, "Does that mean that we are going to keep having deaths?"

Harry folded his hands together. "Yes, that is the most likely case. But the early process modifications, after the first two cases appeared, greatly improved the odds of not getting cancer. However, some of the people who were previously exposed will likely become ill. That's why it is important for all of you to continue with the X-ray and medical lab tests. I wish I could tell you that everything will be okay, but I can't."

"I sure don't like what you said, but I liked the way you put it," Plaid Shirt said, grabbing the whiskey bottle and pouring some into a glass. "That's the first straight talk I've heard. Have a shot, Mr. Schoen." There were several nods around the table.

"Make it Harry. This topic makes shots of whiskey a good idea." He gulped the glass empty and quickly followed the burning of the cheap rye with a pull of beer.

The front door of the house banged open and shut, and a wobbly figure of a man entered and leaned against the doorframe. He instantly focused suspicious eyes on Harry. "Who's this?" he demanded.

Several voices started to explain, only to be cut off: "Some fucking shyster from the company here to soft soap the dumb Polacks. Get your ass out of here, before I throw you out!" He lurched toward Harry. Two of the burlier men intercepted him.

Lorraine jumped up. "I'm sorry, Mr. Schoen. This is my brother, Stosh. Stanley, Mr. Schoen is an invited guest in my house."

"Your house?" he spluttered. "You mean my father's house, before this bastard poisoned him."

"I think I'd better leave now," Harry whispered to Lorraine. "I'll call tomorrow."

"Okay, Mr. Schoen."

"Make it Harry."

"Okay, Harry." He departed with nods to all, and made it a point to slowly don his blazer and walk to the front door as several men continued to restrain Stanley Zdanowski.

———•◦•———

A few days later, Harry hurried down Sixth Street toward the large limestone and brick building on the corner of Walnut Street. Built during the Roaring Twenties, it had been the corporate headquarters of the once formidable Curtis Publishing Company, a now-defunct Philadelphia institution. The company had an illustrious past, from its beginnings as publisher of The Pennsylvania Gazette, founded by the source of much of what is good in Philadelphia, Benjamin Franklin. At its peak, Curtis had been one of the top media companies in the world, best known for its flagship magazine, *The Saturday Evening Post.*

Harry entered the lobby where, although Curtis had long since disappeared from the corporate scene, the building owner had installed an exhibit of covers of old Saturday Evening Post editions. Norman Rockwell's idealized illustrations stirred nostalgic feelings in Harry. It wasn't Rockwell's art that moved him, but the comments they made about American mores. One painting transfixed Harry and he stood still staring at it: Rockwell's famous depiction of an idealized family gathered at the Thanksgiving Day dinner table. Harry had been the boy, and now was the father carving the turkey.

His reverie was interrupted by a voice near his ear. "Grand paintings, are they not, Mr. Schoen?" He turned to look at a man in a rumpled suit, with his shirt stretched tightly across a gut that sagged over his belt.

"Yes, bona fide Americana. It's a little too crowded in here. Let's go into the lobby and find a bench."

They sat on a marble bench before a huge, magnificent Tiffany glass mosaic rendering of a Maxfield Parrish painting, "The Dream Garden."

Sean Ryan was a retired Philadelphia police detective, now a private investigator. He pulled a small, dog-eared notebook from his inside coat pocket, licked his fingers, and began flipping the pages while reciting:

"Stanley Zdanowski, a.k.a. Stosh. Mother died when he was nine; sister Lorraine, three years older, mostly raised him; top five percent of his class at North Catholic High; letter in baseball; no arrests; two years in the army—infantry division in Germany as a mortar crewman, made corporal-honorable discharge; went to Temple on G.I. Bill for three years pre-med; 3.58 g.p.a, while working part-time as a grocery store clerk at an Acme Market; dropped out after father's death to work full-time; finished his degree at night and applied to all of area medical schools—Temple, Penn, Jefferson, Hahneman, etc. Not accepted. Story goes that he's starting to drink a fair amount now and getting a rep for being a little surly. Broke up with his fiancé a few months ago.

"That's it," said Ryan, flipping his notebook closed. "I could go on digging but I think I won't find anything else. Just another Bridesburg Polack who will live and die there, make a few kids, pay his taxes, get drunk once in awhile at the Pulaski or Pilsudski Club, and have a priest say a Polish mass over his body. Sorry I couldn't get anything useful for you, Mr. Schoen."

"I think you may have Mr. Ryan. Just send your bill. Good day." Harry turned and walked off slowly while his brain chewed over the new information. Maybe he had his key.

Chapter Thirteen

Two Promising New Paths?

For several months, Harry continued on as ombudsman for the plant workers. He made sure that every nagging detail that could be handled by the corporation, or by use of its leverage in the community, was covered. He became a regularly-invited attendee at the workers' council meetings at Lorraine's house. On occasion, when sensitive issues were to be discussed, he would be asked, with embarrassment, to leave the room.

He was accepted as a straight shooter, except by the suspicious and surly Stosh. For his part, Harry felt an honest, growing rapport with the group. The Poles of the area were a friendly, generous, industrious lot, given to lusty living. They had a saying that, when invited to one of their homes, you should show up having to knock with your elbows because your arms were laden with gifts. Harry took the cue and often brought pastries or a bottle of Canadian Club rye.

The group now had legal counsel, but Harry avoided contact with him or discussions of legal topics. Fortunately for Schopfer, they had signed up with a local attorney who was wily, but considering some of the powerhouse law firms that were available in Phila-delphia—none of which would have been in any hurry to resolve anything—it could have been far worse for the corporation.

Most importantly, he had gained the trust of Lor-raine. His grief over each worker's death was genuine and his efforts to console each widow at each funeral he attended were appreciated by all, save Stosh.

Meanwhile, an unspoken attraction was growing between Harry and Lorraine. He stifled his feelings out of respect for the business nature of their connec-tion, his moribund marriage, and the seventeen-year age gap, of which he now was acutely sensitive. She had her own misgivings. She knew Harry was mar-ried, although she suspected it was flawed—he rarely spoke of Nancy. She was also inhibited by his social position: a wealthy, high-level executive's interest in a secretary was a cliché. In spite of her growing trust in his integrity, she harbored a flicker of doubt about his motives.

Harry tried but failed to get Ernst or Graber to go to the plant and speak directly to the men. Both cited legal concerns, ignoring Harry's advice that all they had to do was state their sincere grief and regret for the tragedy and commiserate with the men who would soon fall ill and die. Harry knew this would have been deeply appreciated and do much to heal the breach. But they wouldn't budge. He concluded that neither man had the guts to do the dirty work, and left it to the assistant plant manager, who both the workers and Harry disliked.

Harry hated their moral cowardice, while he was

left to face the dying men and their weeping families.

Suspicion was added to his resentment by a newspaper report that, during the time Ernst served as chairman of the Pennsylvania Manufacturers' Association, Robert had strongly and successfully lobbied that group and the Pennsylvania Legislature for a law that made it extremely difficult for workers to sue a fellow employee or executive of their firm for negligence. He had done so with the assistance of a senior lawyer employed by the Schopfer Corporation. With the changes in the law, workers were largely restricted to Workers Compensation payments. This probably had not been Bobby's idea, but he had been the willing agent for it.

From the timing of his lobbying, it was clear that he had to have been aware of the "plant problem," an outrageous conflict of interest. This was the same Robert who donated millions of dollars to charity? Harry began to reassess his opinion of the Schopfer brothers.

———•••———

One day, when Nancy called Harry to tell him that she was unable to join him for dinner and a concert by the Philadelphia Orchestra, Harry gave in to impulse and called Lorraine. She resisted at first, but Harry won her over with his blandishments, the allure of a fancy dinner, and her desire to see the Academy of Music and have a chance to hear an Ormandy performance.

She insisted on meeting him at the restaurant, as she wanted to avoid being seen by her coworkers in his company when there was no meeting of the council. Harry selected Mitchell's, a small supper club on Camac Street, an intimate alley in Center City, with a pianist. She arrived on time, wearing a sea-green, off-the-shoulder satin cocktail gown.

Sitting at the bar facing the door, Harry's heart leaped. "Wow!" he said to himself. The gown beautifully complimented her eyes, and it was just short enough to display her shapely calves.

The program featured works by Beethoven and Stravinsky, who'd been a personal friend of Ormandy's. Afterward, they stopped back at Mitchell's for a cocktail to discuss the program. Neither wanted the evening to end. They agreed that Stravinsky was interesting, but the final score was Beethoven twenty-seven, Stravinsky six. Harry teased Lorraine that she would have given Stravinsky a higher score if his name had ended with an 'i.'

When the hour of decency had come and past, she refused to let him escort her home. Although she assured him that the elevated train and bus were a perfectly respectable way to get home, Harry insisted on putting her in a cab and paying and tipping the driver in advance. It had been his best evening in months.

———•+•———

The concerns of the Bridesburg workers and Harry's commitment to them fed his disgruntlement toward the Schopfers. He was chagrined when he and Nancy were obligated to attend the opening of the old Pine Street Theater as the invited guests of Robert and Zelda. The Schopfer family had poured millions into a lavish restoration of the theater, while they were firing senior employees and resisting compensation for the Bridesburg cancer victims.

The restoration money flowed through one of the family's semi-anonymous charitable trusts, and made a worthy addition to the redevelopment of Center City's cultural life. It also provided a focus for one of Robert's daughters, a sickly and unattractive young lady. The restoration included a private glassed-in area for the family and their friends.

Harry respected the Schopfer's right to spend their money as they wished, but he couldn't help calculating that the costs of the theater project roughly equaled the initial savings to the company from the BOB program. Under the circumstances, the champagne seemed inappropriately festive. He knocked it back like medicine.

Nancy, on the other hand, enjoyed being escorted into the private sanctum, and dove in to the shrill and brittle dialogue. She looked stunning in her evening gown, which brought Harry down even further. How far their marriage had fallen.

Likewise, his career had lost its luster. The constant reminder of the impending deaths of the plant workers he had come to know and respect tore at his soul, and his sleep was marked by troubling dreams. Flannel Shirt was the latest to be told that his chest X-rays showed spots. Now known to Harry as Hank

Majewski, Flannel Shirt announced his death sentence without an eye blink.

On the home front, Harry missed Babs and her ebullient spirit. The house had become a museum, with everything perfectly arranged and polished and dead. Only when Ellen whirled through with his precious grandson did his mood lighten.

Masturbation was a poor second to lovemaking as a release for his sexual tensions. Harry, in spite of his experiences, remained at heart a romantic. He often fantasized about Marie, but was surprised to find his focus returning to Nancy, sleeping just down the hall. But he could not, would not, make that journey. Once he'd made an important decision, he had learned that it was better to avoid looking back.

Lately, Lorraine—she of the long shapely legs—had begun to occupy his fitful dreams. He had always been a leg man, admiring of lanky movie stars such as Alexis Smith, Ava Gardner, Dorothy Mallone, and the incomparable Cyd Charise. Neither Nancy nor Marie had ranked very high on that scale. He kept letting trivial things such as intelligence and humor get in the way.

He took another gulp of champagne, which was beginning to lift his mood a bit.

On his way from one insincere handshake to another, Robert passed by and smiled at Harry. "I'm pleased to see that you're enjoying yourself."

"Yes sir, a beautiful restoration, I'm sure your daughter will have many happy moments here."

"Well, you know how it is with dads and daughters, they— Whoops, excuse me, Harry. The Mayor's arrived."

Robert scuttled off to do his civic duty, introducing Nancy to the Mayor and to the theater's artistic director. Nancy would artfully drop these names into her gossip at the next meetings of the garden club, the literary club, the volunteer ladies of the hospital, the bridge club, and the mah-jongg club.

Ernst broke away from a clutch of chattering evening gowns to ask Harry about the workers' council. "Everything seems to be on an even keel, except that one of the men just got some bad news—spots on his chest x-ray. It's doubly unfortunate because he's been a voice of reason to balance the vitriol of Stanley Zdanowski. But, I have a plan on how to neutralize him. I'll need your help."

"Let's discuss it tomorrow over lunch. Stop by my office at noon tomorrow and we'll walk over to the In-Towner Club."

————

Ernst and Harry finished their broiled shad and roe without having gotten to the business at hand. Harry knew what he was doing and was delighted when Ernst became impatient as Harry peered deeply into his second pony of Johnny Walker Black on the rocks, swirling it between sips.

Ernst finally said, "You mentioned a plan about the...um...plant problem?" Ernst never talked about "workers' deaths."

"Yes sir. It's a two-parter. First I want to try to

neutralize Stanley Zdanowski. He's a burr that undoes half of each step forward. When he's out of the way, I'll be ready to make a trial close on the workers. I doubt they'll buy it straight out of the chute, but I think it'll be close enough to get them into a discussion among themselves.

"At this point I think their lawyer will up the ante a little to justify his fee, and we can compromise on final terms that would be more favorable than we're likely to get from a Philadelphia jury, or an out of court settlement. It makes sense to avoid the mess and publicity of a trial, either in the press or a courtroom."

"Have you discussed this with Higgins or anyone else?"

"No sir. Only you can accomplish the first part, and only you can approve the second."

"I'm all ears. What's the first part?"

"Get Stanley Zdanowski admitted to Penn's Medical School."

Ernst reddened and began to bluster. "That's ridiculous. I can't do that. I don't have the power to interfere and get some unqualified clod admitted."

"Begging your pardon sir, but hear me out. Ben Franklin specifically chartered Penn to be different from other top universities. He stated that its primary function was to train locals to be community leaders and professionals to benefit the commonwealth. The school has continued to produce more leaders of industry than any other.

"Furthermore, he is quite qualified. He graduated from Temple's pre-med with honors, while working part-time. If he were the son of a Mainline doctor or a native of Madagascar, he would have been in."

"But I can't interfere with their admissions!"

"You're a director emeritus of the school, and your foundations have been generous to Penn. All you need to do is ask that they re-examine his application—consider his humble circumstances, death of both parents, military service to his country, the likelihood that he will stay and serve his community well, and the Herculean efforts he made to get through pre-med. Of course, if they decide to accept him, he will have to perform to continue to merit it."

Ernst sought a different escape. "If he gets in, how is he going to pay for it?"

"Grants and loans from Penn to get him started, and I expect the settlement from the company for his father's death will do the rest. It's important that room and board be included, to get him out of Bridesburg. This can all be accomplished orally sir. No checks, no direct transfers of monies, no records."

"I don't like it," Ernst declared, shifting in his chair. "Pushing someone on a university."

Harry struggled to suppress his anger. "Sir, I need your good offices for the sake of the corporation. It amounts to nothing more than giving a disadvantaged young man a chance, much as we are doing with Tyrone McDuffy." This was an unsubtle slap—Harry was certain that Robert and Ernst had helped Tyrone get into, and through, Penn.

Ernst capitulated with a peevish sigh. "All right, I'll consider it." Harry knew from experience that Ernst would acquiesce, after a face-saving period of "consideration." But he also knew that he had given up valuable ground by drawing Ernst directly into solving the plant problem. Harry would be forgiven only if he brought the whole matter to a reasonably good end.

Warily, Ernst said, "Let's have the second part."

"Well, it's something like this. Some cash up front for the victims' families for pain and suffering. Then we effectively keep the deceased on the payroll, a check each week, just supplementing their Worker's Compensation checks, until they would have reached age sixty-two, at which time their widows receive their early retirement pension checks and are eligible for Social Security.

"It's low cost in that the money is paid out slowly, and of course ceases with the death of the widow. Most of the men who have been exposed to the toxic chemical are in their fifties and it will have strong appeal to them, as their chief concerns are not their own deaths, but what will happen to their wives and kids."

Ernst relaxed, tapping the long ash from his cigar into his ashtray. "I like this second part Harry. We could index the checks to inflation, or to match our plant pay rates as they increase, to add to the appeal. As long as we keep the upfront money low enough."

"An inflation index is really good," Harry pounced. "I don't have an up-front cash figure yet, but it'll have to be big enough to sound like a lot of money to them, and get their lawyer to sign on—so he can collect his percentage up front."

"A most interesting proposal, Harry. Why don't you try it out with Legal first. Go straight to Higgins, then work up a per-employee cost estimate with

Finance. Tell George to crunch the numbers himself, have nothing typed. We can't risk any leaks on this. One item for Higgins is how we can make this binding on those who get ill in the future. Or will this only work with those already affected?"

Harry felt he had crested a peak after a long and exhausting climb.

———•·•———

Ernst returned to his office and buzzed his secretary. "Marge, please have Higgins and George Mac-Farland come to my office ASAP. Let me know when they arrive."

He gazed out the window at Independence Mall, processing his lunch exchange. It appeared to him that Harry was beginning to unravel, drinking more, getting too close to the men, betraying a simmering hostility toward fellow executives. Maybe he's not a real team player after all. In any case, he was going to need close observation to make sure he didn't give the store away on these settlements.

Chapter Fourteen

First Steps on New Paths

I t had been several months since Lorraine excitedly called Harry to tell him that her brother, Stosh, had received a letter from Penn accepting him for the medical school under a community outreach program. The letter explained that this initiative sought out candidates who would promise to serve as general practitioners in their home neighborhoods for at least five years after graduation.

Stosh moved into the dormitory two months later and immediately buried himself in his studies. "It's been a miracle!" she gushed. "He quit drinking and he's turned back into his old, good-natured self again. When he talks about his professors and classmates, he just glows."

The bond between Harry and Lorraine had continued to strengthen. One night after a council meeting at her house, Harry lingered for a drink. His marital disaster and his growing involvement with dying men, widows, and children was beginning to take its toll. Lorraine had noticed a newly haggard look on his face, and more frequent recourse to alcohol. She admired his humanity and concern for the workers.

She decided to take a chance. "Harry, you seem down. Would it help to talk about it?"

"I am, but I'm not good at whining."

"I would call it being human."

Harry took a gulp of his drink. "Well, my marriage is stone cold dead and I feel that much of that is my fault. My job is misery now. Trying to help the workers, while remaining in the good graces of the corporation—I'm between the anvil and the hammer."

She reached out and stroked his hair, then kissed him gently. "I want to comfort you, and in honesty, I must say that I want you to want me."

Harry chuckled. "That's the most warmly received offer of my entire life." They embraced again, and she took his hand and led him to her bedroom.

Harry's pent-up passion made it difficult for him to go slowly and gently, but allowed him to experience two orgasms with explosive force. She was a lovely, modest, almost shy partner. Sweet was the word that came to Harry. The experience of her freed him from his Teutonic cage. Tears flooded his eyes as he stroked her hair while gazing at her long lithe body with a diamond shaped escutcheon at the top of those exquisite legs. Her breasts were lovely small mounds with large areolae. He performed cunnilingus on her like a devout supplicant nearing an altar where his prayers would take him to the gates of paradise.

Harry was in love. He was shocked to discover that he was truly in love for the first time. He thought he had loved truly twice before, but he was now plumbing depths of emotions and involvement he had never experienced. The intensity of the feeling unnerved him—a loss of his precious self-control. Even at the funerals of his parents, he had shed no tears and sought no sympathy, choosing instead to be completely alone with his thoughts. He was now operating in strange new territory without his trusty compass. Harry was uncomfortably lost, but newly alive.

———•+•———

In the months that followed, two more men contracted cancer. Harry decided it was a good time to discuss with the council his "pay-as-you-go" plan—the company would pay as the workers go. He'd wanted to open the negotiations with a sixty-five thousand dollar pain and suffering award, but that had quickly been trimmed by his corporate superiors to thirty-five thousand.

Harry deeply resented the fact that these bean counters never had to look into the faces of the dying men. The proposal got a largely negative reaction from the men, but no one spoke of rejecting it out of hand. The men said they would have to review it with their lawyer, and he would give the formal response to Harry and Allen Higgins, the corporate counsel.

———•+•———

Harry and Lorraine were having dinner the next week at the Three Threes, an intimate bistro. Harry loved how Lorraine laughed and ate. No little teehees, but rather a hearty full laugh. No picking lightly at her meal, but an appreciative savoring of fine food. During the main course, Lorraine raised the topic Harry had been carefully avoiding in their personal conversations.

"The reaction of the men to your proposal is moving from largely negative to somewhat positive. But they have reservations about the low initial payment." She commented with candor, "It's more money than any of us have ever seen at once."

"It isn't necessary for you to inform me, and perhaps better if we just avoid the topic and let the negotiations follow their own course."

"I agree. But there hasn't been much money in my house since the days my father worked while the plant was on four shifts to run twenty-four hours a day, seven days a week, for a couple months."

Harry's interest suddenly perked up. "When was that?"

"Just before it shut down. Apparently they got a huge order from Japan."

Harry frowned, but he said, "Let's finish our Napoleans. Concert time is coming up, and you know the orchestra. If you're late, they close the doors and you have to wait 'til intermission."

Harry sat through the performance oblivious to the music. The company's plants rarely worked twenty-four hour/seven day weeks, except in emergencies, such as a strike at another plant or a massive equipment failure. Also, the products made in Bridesburg were new at the time, and would be expected to slowly climb in sales volumes.

His confidence in the company's moral commitment in dealing with the cancer problem had already been shaken by the newspaper article that revealed Robert's lobbying the state legislature for a change in the labor laws that helped protect Schopfer and its executives from workers' lawsuits. Nor did he like the delay in starting the testing with mice and the slow response to the negative results.

The next day, Harry ordered and reviewed the annual sales figures for the products from the process that employed the deadly dibromomethyl ether. Sales in the Pacific region were now large, but appeared to be small two years after the plant shut down. He closed the ledger. He asked his secretary to get production figures for the products dating back to their launches, years before the cancers had arisen.

She returned with data starting two years after the shut-down. She couldn't find anything earlier. He then asked her to have George MacFarland's finance office compute the net profits based on the data, along with the sales department's projections for future sales going five years out.

His head was churning. What the hell was going on? This company, with its Germanic heritage, probably had kept records going back to the first pound of the first tanning product it ever produced. Things weren't adding up.

Harry and his assistant, Tyrone, were taking a break at a coffee shop near the office, debating the Phillies' prospects for the season, when MacFarland showed up and invited himself to join them. MacFarland congratulated Tyrone on a recent market research presentation he'd made, pronouncing it "concise and punchy."

When it was time to return to the office, MacFarland asked Harry to wait a moment after Tyrone left.

"The profit data you asked for is almost ready," he said. "You should have it later today." He hesitated, then asked, with feigned indifference, "What's the purpose of this exercise? Why did you personally pull the production data?"

"Just estimating the value of the products to the corporation, to compare with the potential costs of the settlement, and to consider a possible worst case cost scenario."

"That's my job," MacFarland said quickly. "I have the figures, so leave it to me. What would constitute a worse case scenario?"

"The workers' lawyer jacks us up to a hundred thousand up front and I make the assumption that I have to apply your forthcoming average projected settlement cost per employee to every production person who was ever exposed to the process."

"My God Harry, you really don't expect them all to die!"

"No, I don't. But you know the allowable inhalation estimate for this carcinogen is now known to be so low that before the shut down, full bottle up, and pressure masks, we must have exceeded that from time to time. I always consider the slippery-pole case in any business situation."

MacFarland shook his head in disbelief. "Listen, it's unnecessary and undesirable for you to make such calculations. In the interest of security, I'm holding all such data personally. I will develop it and review it with you, orally."

"That's fine George, I'm sure you'll do it faster and better than I. Besides, I dreaded doing it myself."

"How many men are you considering to have had possible exposure?"

"For your calculations, assume sixty."

"My God! Sixty?"

"Sixty, George."

"Christ! How can you stand this assignment?"

"I don't know that I can. I guess losing thirty-five men in two hours in Korea was good training," Harry said with an edge in his voice. "At least they died fast, fighting an enemy they could see."

Harry returned to his office, hoping MacFarland had accepted his ruse for digging through old production data.

Chapter Fifteen

Major Discoveries on the New Paths

Harry was not ready to throw in the towel in his efforts to get a copy of the old production figures. He recruited Lorraine, telling her he had an assignment she would have to hold in total secrecy, at the risk of their careers at Schopfer.

She proved herself game. "Tell me what you want."

"I want you to find the production records for the cancer producing products at the plant going back to the beginning. I particularly want them for the years before, during, and after the shut down."

Lorraine knew better than to press Harry for details. But she warned him the records were kept in locked files in the plant manager's office. "It's a busy place during the day, but at night the foremen for each production building are in charge, and they tend to remain at their work stations. Once in awhile they come to the office to get process or reference data. The watchmen make regular passes through all of the buildings."

"Do you know the combinations?"

"I'm not supposed to, but the combinations are changed periodically and Mr. Budd, the plant manager, has trouble remembering them. He keeps a pony in his desk. I know where it is."

"Is there some way you can stay late without drawing attention?"

"Not until the end of the month, when the plant manager has to compile a summary report. If I'm running behind, I stay until I complete a draft to leave on his desk for his approval the next morning."

"Sounds good. You even have a cover story for being alone in his office. I hate to ask you to slink around, but you aren't stealing anything. Just get me copies of those data, and please don't get caught!"

The day Lorraine expected to pull off the caper, Harry waited in his office, pacing the floor. All the clerks and secretaries had gone home for the day, but a few of the managers were still at their desks. Harry loitered near his office door, nervously nodding to people on their way to the elevators. His attention was focused on the silent phone on his desk. It seemed to be taking too long. Harry checked his watch for the hundredth time.

Lorraine said goodnight to Mr. Budd as he headed out the door on his way home. She was annoyed to find one of the building foremen was still in his office, leisurely smoking a cigar and poring over some of the raw data sheets. She went back to her desk and began typing, slowly, a third draft of the report. Finally, she stuck her head in the door to tell the foreman she would be going to the ladies room for a few minutes. "Hey Bob," she said, "do me a favor and take that smelly cigar butt with you. I know you guys can't smoke in the plant, but I get gassed out here."

"Okay Lorraine, sorry about that. I'll be gone by the time you get back. I'll dump the cigar in the men's room. Have a good night."

Lorraine waited just inside the women's room, cracking the door a smidge so she could survey the office. As soon as Bob left, she scurried back and quickly deposited the report draft on Mr. Budd's desk. She had to hurry. The guard was due shortly. She got the combination and opened the file cabinet. She could only find production figures from two years after the shut down.

She pulled files for other product lines and found continuous records. She was trying to figure out why when she was interrupted by footsteps in the hallway. She shoved the folders back into the drawer and closed the door just shy of latching, so there'd be no clicking sound. She plopped herself in Budd's chair and scattered the pages of the report around the desk, just as Bob rounded the jam.

"Still at it Lorraine? I thought I better return this ashtray. Note that I even rinsed it off."

Lorraine laughed to cover her breathlessness. "If I knew you did ashtrays Bob, I would have married you." She stood up and headed toward the door with the foreman just as the watchman stuck his head in.

"God you're quiet," Bob said. "Scared the hell out of me."

"Crepe soles. Makes it easier on my feet," he said. "I log about six miles a night around this plant. Well, I guess we're secure with you two here. Goodnight. I have to keep moving to hit my time keys."

"I'll walk out with you. Ready to leave, Lorraine?"

"You two go ahead. I want to proofread this one more time."

Bob and the watchman departed, and Lorraine's breathing slowly returned to normal. She eased the file drawer closed, spun the dial, and turned off the lights.

An hour later, Harry rolled his station wagon to a stop in front of Lorraine's row house which, small and shabby, now felt more like home than the polished but arid Bucks County house he shared with Nancy. Harry didn't need all the trappings. He considered himself in some ways a minimalist. His office was almost spartan by peer standards. Beyond a few family photographs, there were few clues to the style of the occupant. He enjoyed a few things of high quality, such as his business wardrobe, the orchestra, doctors, education for his children, fine literature, single malt scotches, cigars, and his cabin cruiser on Long Beach Island.

He simply didn't care about most of the other external manifestations of success, such as being seen with the right people in the right places, exotic vacations, belonging to the right clubs, and so on. The only purpose they had served in his life were to pacify

Nancy, and provide a good setting to raise his children. Houses were just bricks and sticks. People counted.

He was disappointed with what Lorraine found. She had confirmed his suspicions that the company had deliberately cleansed the files by comparing the record keeping on other products.

Lorraine greeted him with a kiss and a chilled dry Rob Roy. He sagged into a well-worn easy chair.

"What now?"

"First I need another Rob Roy." She freshened his drink, then he began slowly. "You must trust me completely, and accept that I am going to act in the best interests of the plant men. Can you do that?"

"Three months ago I couldn't. But now I love you and have complete faith in your integrity."

"Three months ago you would have been right not to trust me fully. I'm capable of being very sneaky. For example, I got Stosh admitted to medical school mostly to get him out of my way."

Her eyebrows raised a tad, but she said nothing.

"I like the men, and I grieve with each new case. I'm determined to see that they're treated fairly by the company. If old Hans were still alive, they would be. Ernst, Robert, and Graber don't have the guts to deal straight up with this mess. I'm convinced this was an unintentional problem resulting from human error, and stupidity, crossing the line into criminality."

"Criminal!?"

"After getting the bad news about the virulence of the ether contaminant, the plant was run flat out for two months to produce enough inventory to supply the market while the plant shut down for refitting.

I think the Japanese order was a cover story for the all-out production run. But I can't prove any of it without the production and sales figures, which look like they're gone forever."

"How about the memories of the men, or their widows?"

"That would be embarrassing for the company, but years-old recollections by biased parties in lawsuits would be a tough sell. We need concrete proof, but the people who know the truth are ashamed to admit it."

"What can we do?"

"I could run a bluff, pretend I know more than I do. But there are some excellent poker players to go up against. If they call me, I'm dead. Let me sleep on it. Or, more accurately, toss and turn on it for awhile."

As she watched Harry descend the steps to his car, Lorraine glowed with admiration for him.

———•◆•———

Negotiations with the men proceeded much as Harry had forecast. The workers had bought into the idea of exchanging their lives for the security of their families. They also agreed to small up-front payments for other potentially exposed employees. If they contracted cancer, they would qualify for the full settlement terms. Higgins, the company's chief counsel, had suggested that provision.

Harry recognized that Schopfer was exploiting the workers' modest circumstances and familial concerns. The hard point would be the size of the pain and suffering payment. The best Harry could do was to address their worries about the financial support of their wives and children. No amount of money could compensate the men for coughing their lungs out.

The men's lawyer, Tom Novakowski, seemed like a decent, honest attorney, direct billing them for his hours, and a ten percent contingency fee on the value of the settlement. But he'd been fighting a rear-guard action. The workers had adopted a "one for all, and all for one" position. He was asking for one hundred thousand dollars per man for pain and suffering.

Higgins and the firm's outside counsel, a prestigious center city corporate litigation firm, had developed a plan that would tie the workers up in court for years. Harry had recommended offering sixty-five thousand dollars to bring about a quick settlement. But Schopfer was insisting that fifty thousand was a maximum. The men had dug in their heels.

During one of the corporate meetings, Harry pointed out that sixty-five thousand dollars was only about five years pay for the workers. "I wonder," he mused, "how many of us sitting here would be willing to exchange our lives for five years pay." A stony silence greeted the remark, finally broken by Graber. "The stockholders wouldn't think we were worth it." That elicited a relieved chuckle from the men, but Harry caught Graber and Ernst exchanging a knowing glance.

He could feel himself gradually being isolated, but he held the only trusted link to the workers, so he was still useful. While the loyalty he felt toward Schopfer eroded, his relationship with his assistant, Tyrone, flourished. There was such a level of trust between them that Tyrone began reporting to Harry every time headhunters approached him with job offers. Harry acted as a sounding board, noting the benefits and drawbacks of each offer. Tyrone's own characterization of many of them was that they were high on the money, but low on the job: "It's obvious they decided to go get themselves a nigger and prop him up in the window." Harry had a similar feeling about how he was being used as a stage prop by Schopfer Chemical. He resented being the company stooge.

———————

The negotiations with the men had been drifting for weeks when he got a phone call from Lorraine.

"I think I found some important things and I can't wait to discuss them with you. Can you stop by tonight?"

Harry heard the tremor of excitement in her voice, and gave a quick yes for seven o'clock. He fished for details, but Lorraine wasn't biting.

"In the flesh only. I'll have some iced oysters, crab salad, and champagne. I expect we'll be two happy people."

He had trouble concentrating on his work as the clock seemed to slow down. He made the perfunctory call home to say he'd be late. He knew that Nancy knew that he was having an affair. And she knew that he was unconcerned that she knew. The ties that had bound

Harry to his world were quickly coming undone.

Lorraine's door flew open before he'd gotten to the steps. She greeted him with a passionate, wet kiss and a glass of cheap champagne.

Next she served an icy blue point oyster. He drained his glass, seized her by the waist, pushed her down on the couch, and tickled her. "Vee haff vays to make you talk."

"Okay you Kraut. I'll talk."

She reached over the arm of the sofa and produced an old shoebox that had been sitting on the floor. She cradled it in her arms as she explained, "After my father died, Stosh and I left his bedroom pretty much the way it was, except for donating his clothing and some personal stuff to the Saint Vincent DePaul Society. After that, we closed the door and the room's been just like that, all these years.

"My father was meticulous. He kept all his records, even his electric bills and old pay stubs, all neatly stored on the closet floor in shoeboxes.

"In one shoebox were years of pay stubs, including the year of the plant closure." She dealt them out on the coffee table like a deck of cards. "Look, Harry. See how they trace a fairly even line of weekly numbers, until the eight before the closure when they spike, and then fall back to the previous period. I checked with some of the widows. Two of them also had their husband's stubs. Same thing.

"That's proof! The plant was running on overtime! " Her eyes gleamed with excitement.

Harry was impressed. They were a good team. "Now I understand why Ernst and Graber couldn't face the men. They knew about this!"

"Not finished, Tarzan," she laughed. "Jane think, Where they put all this product? Check freight bills. Not find any for Japan. Find several for loads going to a public warehouse in Charlotte, North Carolina, rather than our own warehouses. A public warehouse that we had never used before, nor since. The bills start about seven weeks before the shut-down, build, and then diminish in size each month after the closure, and finally end six months after the re-start."

It was all coming together, in Harry's loins. He couldn't resist a woman with good legs and great brains.

They made love right there on the floor, making it last with pauses for champagne. Afterward, exhausted, they snuggled on the couch until Harry stirred and said he had to get going. Lorraine pouted as he pulled on his clothes, now all business.

"I have to go. We've got work to do. You need to tell the widows to hold on to the pay stubs and other financial records, that they might be needed to compute a future financial settlement." Lorraine sat up, grabbed a pencil and a scrap of paper from the coffee table, and scribbled some notes.

"Then you have to get copies of those warehouse bills and swap them for the originals, which you will bring home. Then, together with the pay records, you'll put them in a safety deposit box. That's our insurance policy, the nuclear option.

"Then I can dictate the terms of the final settlement to the company, at which point, I will resign to, as they say, pursue personal interests."

Lorraine shot Harry a slack-jawed look.

"You'd destroy your career? Just like that?"

He slipped his feet into his loafers like a pair of punctuation marks. "It's already destroyed. Ernst and Graber are on to me. I can feel it. What they haven't counted on is that I don't give a shit."

Lorraine got up and wrapped herself in a robe. "What about your wife, and your girls?"

"Divorce. I'm tired of living a sham. If it's grow-up time for the girls, so be it." His whole being felt flooded with purpose.

Lorraine gave him a lingering hug. "I feel so bad. Look at the price you're paying. Is it worth it?"

Harry stroked her hair. "I've made so many 'reasonable compromises' that I have fractionated myself to death. This may be my last, best chance to be a whole man again!"

Chapter Sixteen

Break-ups Are Hard To Do

Harry had his divorce discussion with Nancy who, in one sitting, raced through the stages from shock through self-pity to revenge. When she got to, "What will happen to me?" Harry's first thought was how it was a perfect moment to quote Rhett Butler. But he didn't need to be cruel to Nancy. She was making it hard enough on herself. As Marie had pointed out, "A broken love affair is like a horse with a broken leg. The kindest thing is to shoot it."

"I'll make you pay!" Nancy stormed around the kitchen, slamming cabinets and drawers as she put away the breakfast dishes.

Harry shrugged and sipped his coffee. "No problem. Have your lawyer call me. I won't contest the divorce. You can have the house and all that goes with it, half of all my pension and investment funds, the Caddy, half of my severance package from Schopfer, and I'll even pay for Babs's college costs.

"All I want is the cabin cruiser and the station wagon, which I will use this weekend to haul away my clothing and personal effects. I'll pack a bag to hold me till the weekend, and move to a hotel tonight."

"Severance package? You've been fired?"

"Not yet. I'm going to resign first."

"Resign your job! Divorce! What the hell's wrong with you! Have you lost your mind?"

"Why don't you tell your friends I had a mid-life crisis? That ought to get you off the hook. I prefer to think of it as finally being myself."

Nancy stopped fussing and leaned over the sink, head bowed as if in thought. The fight seemed to visibly drain out of her. When she looked up, her eyes were pink.

"What happened to us, Harry? Everything we wished for when we got married we've achieved."

"Be careful what you wish for, right? Maybe we wished for the wrong things."

"Couldn't we just try a little harder?" Harry couldn't take the wounded look in her eyes any longer. He had to pull the trigger.

"I've got to pack."

As he climbed the stairs, he thought of Oscar Wilde: "All men kill the thing they love...some strangle with the hands of lust, some with the hands of gold: the kindest use a knife, because the dead so soon grows cold...." He had used a sword on Nancy, but he realized that his lust for career success and power had driven her into the shallow lust for gold.

When he was packed and ready to leave, he found Nancy sitting at the bottom of the staircase, bawling. He sat next to her and gently pulled her to him. "We accomplished a lot together. Two great daughters, and now a grandson to love.

"We started out as a team but each of us has gone

so far down our separate trails that we're shouting distance apart. Look, if you need to talk or have any problems, call me." He kissed the top of her head, stood, and walked out, closing the door softly behind him.

———•·•———

Harry requested a late Friday afternoon meeting with Ernst and Allen Higgins. In spite of the stress, Harry and Higgins had developed mutual respect. Together they had done all the heavy lifting in trying to resolve this sordid depressing business.

Ernst tried to seize the initiative. "Harry, you look beat. I want you to know I really appreciate your efforts with the plant problem. Maybe you should take some time off, take a vacation."

"Thanks for your concern, but I expect this entire affair will be wrapped up tonight in my meeting with the workers' council. After that I expect I'll have lots of time to myself."

Ernst's cigar froze in mid-air and he shot Harry a sharp look, with narrowed eyes. "A wrap up? This evening? Has there been a breakthrough in the negotiations?"

"You might say that. Especially after I tell the men that you and Robert have taken personal charge of the situation and decided to resolve it, and that you two decided that haggling was out of character with your father's principles, and you agreed to personally authorize payments of a hundred grand."

Higgins stared at Harry, shaking his head

slightly.

Ernst stabbed at the ashtray with his cigar. "You... You just...decided that...by yourself!?"

"There's more," Harry pushed on. "You and Robert have also decided that out of respect for your father and his rapport with the loyal workers of the Philadelphia plant, you will match the company's awards with your personal funds, which will be placed in investment accounts for each victim's heirs."

Ernst slammed his palm on the table top. "Harry, I'm afraid the strain has gotten to you. I'm going to put you on medical leave. In fact, I'll have my driver take you home right now. I'll call Nancy to tell her you're on your way."

"No thanks," Harry said. "What I just described is exactly what's going to transpire."

Ernst was turning red. Higgins stilled him with a raised hand. "Harry, what's going on?"

"I have concrete evidence that this company deliberately ran the Bridesburg plant when it knew, absolutely, that it should have been shut down."

"That's ridiculous!" Spit flew from Ernst's lips. "The strain of this assignment has unglued you. Absurd!"

"Worse than absurd," Harry replied. "Unconscionable. Maybe even criminal. The plant was run full out, twenty-four hours a day, seven days a week, for two months before the shut down."

Ernst sank back in his chair. "Okay, it was. But that was just a coincidence. We had a large order from a Japanese customer."

Harry ignored Ernst's lie. "Don't you think it's

strange, in a company that still has the first invoice for the first sale it ever made, that all the production data from that period have disappeared?"

Higgins rubbed his chin. "Is that true, Ernst?"

Ernst waved his hand. "Oh, I never know about such details."

Harry folded his hands and turned to Higgins. "All the records for products other than those associated with the cancers are freely accessible."

Higgins frowned and looked at Ernst. "If those records disappeared, that would be very serious."

"There's more, Allen," Harry continued. "I can prove that the products were not shipped to Japan, but rather were stored in a public warehouse in North Carolina. Imagine what would happen if this information were to find its way into the hands of the workers' lawyer, or to the investigative reporters at the *Daily Press*, or a district attorney who wants to be mayor?

"After the press conflagration, what kind of settlements do you think a jury might award, or what kind of settlement might the workers be able to extract?" Harry pointed out the wall of windows in Ernst's office, toward City Hall with its crowning statue of William Penn.

"As old Ben Franklin once said, 'Three can keep a secret, provided two of them are dead.' In this case, spilling the beans could also mean criminal charges. How about reckless and willful endangerment, or conspiracy?"

Ernst propped his elbows on the table and buried his face in his hands. Higgins broke the uncomfortable silence. "I didn't know about this. I thought I was representing good people who had done something dumb." He turned to Ernst whose long face shocked Harry. Ernst had never let his guard down.

"This is a dog shit situation," Higgins scowled at Ernst. "The more you stir it the worse it smells. You have no choice but to take Harry's deal. This can't go beyond this room. You've always struck me as a man of your word, Harry. You've got to give it now."

"You have my word, as long as the men are taken care of. And one more thing," he said, turning to Ernst. "I want to hear it from your mouth. How the hell did this happen?"

Ernst stared into his lap, the scolded schoolboy.

"Ernst?" Higgins prodded.

Ernst sighed. "We got a preliminary oral report about how badly the carcinogenicity testing was going. The lab said it would take two more months to finish the tests and issue a written report. The marketing people got wind of this and were pissed off. They had some big Japanese prospects who were in the middle of trials with the products. Any hint of a supply problem could have killed the sales.

"They convinced the production people to say that, with the process improvements we had already put into place, we would be okay. Later, when the report came in with a low air tolerance level, I realized what we'd done."

The worst part about it, Harry thought, was that it made perfect sense. Once you throw out the old values, any behavior can be rationalized.

"Okay," Harry said. "Some good people made some bad decisions. Now you keep your word to make it right, and I'll keep my word to keep it quiet." He stood to leave, pulling an envelope from his jacket pocket.

"One last detail. Here is my letter of resignation, effective Monday morning."

Ernst looked at Harry with pained eyes. "I want you to know that this affair has destroyed my self-esteem. It'll be with me the rest of my life. I'm sorry I dragged you down with me. I hate to see you leave the company."

"The company left me, Ernst. You're reaping what you sowed. I used to be proud to work here, but now I'm betting on myself.

"You have money and power. You have plenty of time to do good with the rest of your life. As for the men who got sick and died, I can tell you from personal experience that their ghosts will be with you for the rest of your days."

They shook hands, then Higgins walked Harry to the elevator. "You have my solemn vow that this will be done right."

"I have no doubt of that, Allen."

"So, now that you've slain the dragon, what's next?"

"I'm going to float around the Atlantic Ocean on my cruiser, pretend to fish, enjoy the salt air, drink my Scotch, and look at the waves and sky. When fall comes, I'll follow the sun to the Florida Keys. Like we used to say in the service, 'mox nix'."

"Huh?"

"In Korea, most of the officers and NCO's had served in Germany in the Second World War. It was a catchall expression, m-o-x n-i-x. It's a corruption of a German expression—*machts nichts*. It means 'it makes nothing,' or 'who cares,' or 'so what.' It's what a German says when he shrugs his shoulders." Harry shrugged and winked at Higgins as the elevator doors closed between them.

———•·•———

The men and widows left Lorraine's house that night in good spirits. All had shaken Harry's hand, and a few had asked him to express their appreciation directly to the Schopfer brothers. One old-timer noted that acorns don't fall far from the tree. "Those boys did just what the old man woulda done," he said with pride.

Harry thought Hans would have made sure it didn't get as bad as it had, and he would have personally grieved with the men, and been quick and generous with settlements.

A thin and stooped Hank Majewski—Flannel Shirt—was the last to leave. He took Harry's hand between his calloused palms. "I gave up on the tooth fairy years ago, but now I'm not so sure. I don't know how the hell you did this, but you've taken a great load off me. I can go my way, now that my wife and kids are protected."

Lorraine hugged Hank and saw him to the door. When she came back she poured themselves drinks and settled beside Harry on the sofa. "Well, you won. Now what?"

"I'm newly unemployed. Between giving Nancy the store and cutting off my income, I'm well on my way to becoming a beach bum.

"But then again, my burn rate is going way down. Gasoline and docking fees, but no income or real estate taxes, and lots of fish dinners. I've got enough for a few years 'til I decide what I want to be when I grow up."

Lorraine waited expectantly, drink in mid-air.

"Oh, you mean, what about us, right? Okay, I flat out love you, but my head is screwed up, and I need time to think. Anyway, I'm too old."

"You're not."

"Maybe not today, but tomorrow. You deserve children. Can I travel that course again?" He shrugged.

"Just one would be nice." She frowned when she saw he wasn't kidding.

"Being a parent is a lifetime sentence, no time off for good behavior. It's the one decision in life that can't be changed or erased." Lorraine looked away, her eyes stinging with emotion.

"No fair crying," Harry joked. "I can't win against that."

She dabbed at the corners of her eyes with her sleeve. "You're right, it is unfair. That's why I'm doing it."

"Time out. I'm leaving for the shore to get my boat painted, docked, and ready to go. Give me two weeks and then come down. If we can survive a weekend of living together on my cruiser, complete with fishing, maybe there is a chance for us."

"I love fishing!"

"You love fishing?"

"I used to love to go fishing with my father, but we hardly ever caught anything."

"You're upsetting my whole philosophy about men versus women. Shopping is to women what fishing is to men. Women enjoy shopping even if they don't buy anything, while men only go to buy. Men enjoy fishing, even if they catch nothing, while women are bored out of their skulls if nothing happens for an hour."

"Well, too bad for your philosophy, because I hate shopping and love fishing."

Harry sighed. He had a few wiggles left in him, but he knew he was hooked.

The End

Epilogue

Willis Brophy, dressed in a linty, baggy corduroy suit and reeking of cigarette smoke, limped into his editor's office at the *Philadelphia Times*. He was officially retired, but contributing articles now and then when he felt like it.

It had been thirty years since he wrote his investigative series on the suspicious deaths of Schopfer Chemical Company workers. It was only natural that the paper asked him to write the company's obituary. He looked forward to the task, thinking how true it was that revenge is a dish best served cold.

He tossed his papers on the editor's desk. "Here's the bullshit for the public." He sat down with a heavy thump.

"After all these years, you've still got that story under your skin. What's up with that?"

"It ended, but it still smelled rotten. I could never get to the bottom of the story. And all those funerals. I actually went and bought myself a black suit so I wouldn't stick out. Haven't used it since."

The editor had handled thousands of stories for the paper so he only knew about Brophy's groundbreaking coverage by reputation: he'd won a Pulitzer for his work.

Brophy made no move to leave and the editor sensed the old war horse was in a reflective mood. "So, how do you see the series shaping up? Time Passes Schopfer By?"

He opened a desk drawer and pulled out a half-bottle of rye and two glasses. "Join me?" Brophy raised three fingers, then watched the editor pour.

"Well, at one time Schopfer was a first-rate out-fit—when old Hans, the founder, ran it. But it decayed rapidly after he was gone. I was going to write a book about it, but you know, I always was an old fire horse, ready to charge out when the bell rings for the next story."

The editor rocked back in his chair. "Sometimes they were even true."

"Right! So, Hans was a pyramid builder. You know, the kind that builds companies as monuments to themselves. If you can contribute a few stones to the pyramid, they will be effusive in their affection. If you can't help them, they'll ignore you to death.

"Then, when they've grown large and rich—and large far outweighs rich—or maybe the fires are bank-ing with age, they become pillars of the community and get schools and hospital wings named after them.

"Hans subjugated those around him, including his sons. His death left a vacuum that was filled by less talented people. The company coasted for a time, but three men came together and really screwed it up.

"Ernst, who had inherited the reins, made Dr. Bel-lington head of R&D, the wellspring of the company's success. Bellington walked and talked a good game, but he was in love with his ideas, and hated all others.

He drove the best lab men away.

"Suspect number two was also recruited by Ernst. He was an energetic, smooth-talking finance guy, Joe Graber, brought on as president. He was one of the then-new breed of corporate leaders with an M.B.A. in finance from Harvard and experience in the overseas subsidiaries, but lacked technical and marketing skills. Both of the guys Ernst brought in wanted to leave their mark on the company. Thus was formed the unholy trinity."

"So, how did the geniuses screw it up?"

"Well as I got it from retirees, under Bellington, research that had not been under his control before his promotion was cut to provide funds for his pet projects. Graber loved to brag to financial analysts about what he was going to achieve. Old Hans had ignored the Street, simply churning out steady profits that pushed the stock from ten dollars a share to a split-adjusted nine hundred.

"Graber lusted for major new developments from Research, which, of course, could only be achieved with Bellington's brilliance. They plunged into a disastrous diversification program supported by inept marketing and insanely optimistic profit projections. It was a recipe for disaster, and it worked.

"The company stumbled along, bought its way out of that ether mess at Bridesburg, and slowly sank in its industry standing. The stock languished until Ernst had his fatal heart attack. Then Robert was forced out, the kids took over, and sold the company off to that German outfit. I think Robert's dead now, too.

"So, in the end, Hans Schopfer's pyramid, constructed in the twentieth century, was de-constructed in the twenty-first, and is now covered by the sands of time. Maybe it was fitting that an independent firm, founded in Germany, should return there to die as an independent firm."

"So the turning point was the cancer deaths at Bridesburg?" The editor freshened both their glasses as the City Hall clock struck four times.

"More or less. But what made it interesting to me at the time were the rumors that an up-and-comer in the company, another kraut named Schoen, sabotaged the Schopfer brother's efforts to sweep the thing under the carpet. One minute they were trying to get the victims to settle for Workers' Compensation plus a few bucks. But then, on a dime, they turned around and offered generous settlements, including personal money out of the pockets of Ernst and Robert.

"One of the funerals I went to was for a guy named Majewski. His widow said Schoen had somehow made it happen. Schoen was there, and even said a few words. After the service, I tried to get him to talk but he wasn't giving it up. I poked around on it for a few months, talked to some of the surviving workers and their spouses, but nobody would own up to a damn thing. You'd think they'd be mad at the company and vent, but they didn't even do that."

"Too bad," the editor mused, distracted by a pile of articles a clerk had just dropped on his desk.

"It galls me to do it, but the series will make the company and the family look pretty good. But my nose still twitches like a rabbit's when the Bridesburg affair comes to mind." He shrugged. "Oh well, mox nix, as they say."

"Huh?"

"Mox nix, or machts nichts. It's an expression some of the Bridesburg people used. It's German, means 'makes nothing,' or 'doesn't matter.'"

The two men clinked their glasses and drained them.